A NICE DERA... S

By the same author

ELLIS PETERS

A Nice Derangement of Epitaphs

Futura

A Futura Book

First published in Great Britain in 1965
by William Collins, Sons & Co. Ltd

This edition published in 1988 by
Futura Publications, a Division of
Macdonald & Co (Publishers) Ltd,
London & Sydney

ISBN 0 7088 3751 4

Printed and bound in Great Britain by
Hazell Watson & Viney Limited
Member of BPCC plc
Aylesbury Bucks

Futura Publications
A Division of
Macdonald & Co (Publishers) Ltd
Greater London House
Hampstead Road
London NW1 7QX
A Pergamon Press plc company

CONTENTS

MRS. MALAPROP: Sure, if I reprehend anything in this world it is the use of my oracular tongue, and a nice derangement of epitaphs!

SHERIDAN: *The Rivals*

CHAPTER I

WEDNESDAY

THE BOY in the sea was in difficulties, that was plain from the first moment Dominic clapped eyes on him. Only a seal could possibly navigate off the Dragon's Head in a tide like this one, racing out on the ebb with the impetus of an express train, checking and breaking back again like hammers on the toothed rocks, lashing out right and left in bone-white spray, and seething down through the wet sand in deep clawmarks, with a hissing like the old serpent of legend striking and missing his prey. For a mile off the point, far into deep water greener than emeralds, the sea boiled. Nobody in his senses swam there in an ebbing tide.

He cupped his hands and yelled, and the bobbing head, a small cork tossed in a cauldron of foam, heaved clear of the spray for an instant and turned towards him a pallor which must be its face. He yelled again, and peremptorily waved the swimmer inshore. The clamour of the ebb off the point might well have carried his voice away, but the gesture was seen and understood. And ignored. The head vanished in foam, and reappeared tossing off spray, battling doggedly outward.

Dominic looked round wildly for someone else to take the decision from him, but there was nobody. This wasn't the populous Maymouth side of the Dragon, but the bleak bay of Pentarno on the northern side, and tea-time of a fine but blowy day, when nobody frequented those sandy wastes. Mile upon mile of drifted sand on his right hand, and inland, beyond the processional dunes, the first green of pasture and gold and brown of stubble; and on his left the craggy bastions of the Dragon's Head, running out to sea in a grapeshot of scattered rocks, the cliff paths a six-strand necklace above him, a tapering crescent of pebbles below. Not a local in sight to take the load from him. And if he didn't make up his mind quickly it might be too late. Better make a fool of yourself than watch some other fool kid drown himself before your eyes.

Oh, damn! Whether he was in trouble or not——!

Dominic launched himself from the path and went down the last slope of thinning grass and shale in a long, precarious slither, to arrive upright but staggering in the grey pebble shelf under the rocks, just clear of the hissing water. It was falling rapidly now, and this was no very good place to go in, but he had no choice. He shed his shirt and slacks, kicked off his sandals, and waded into water that ran back before him, snatching its last fringes away from his toes in a scurry of foam. He overtook it, felt his way as fast as he dared down the broken slippery descent, took one last rapid sighting, and struck out strongly towards the boy in the sea.

The first stages were easy, and he knew his own capabilities and could trust himself in this much of a sea, even if his own experience had been gained in the makeshift river-and-swimming-bath conditions of a land-locked county. But the currents off these rocks were something nobody would willingly venture in a fast ebb like this, and the thought of the jagged teeth ripping up the water into oil-green ribbons clung in his mind through every minute of that swim. Half a mile northward, and the mild, long rollers would be sliding innocently down the level sand, as harmless as the ripples in a baby's bath. Here he had a fight on his hands.

He dug his shoulders into it, head low, edging away from the rocks with every stroke. Once he hoisted himself out of the trough to take a fresh sighting, and found the boy by the glimpse of a slender arm flung clear of the water for an instant. Nearer than Dominic had expected. And perhaps still clear of the treacherous pull of the rocks. Maybe he'd known what he was doing, after all. Maybe he was one of the harbour kids, bred from some ancestry involving fish, and did this every afternoon for fun.

But no, that wouldn't do. The harbour kids simply didn't

go in off the point, they had too much sense. The ones who can do nearly everything never push their luck to the last rim, because they don't have to prove anything, they know.

Well, if this kid was the strongest swimmer on the North Cornish coast, he was coming ashore now, if his rescuer had to knock him out to bring him.

The sea flung them together almost unexpectedly in the end; two startled faces, open-mouthed, hair streaming water, glared at each other out of focus, six inches of ocean racing between them hard and green as bottle-glass. Dominic caught at a thin, slippery arm, and gripped it, pulling the boy round to lie against his body. The boy opened his mouth to yell, and choked on water, rolling helplessly for a moment; and then he was being towed strongly back towards the shore, and seemed to have lost all command of his own powers at the shock of such an indignity. He recovered almost as quickly, and suddenly he was a fury. He jerked himself free and tried to dive under his rescuer, but he had met with a resolution as grim as his own. The plunging head was retrieved painfully by its wet hair, and clipped smartly on the ear into the bargain. The sea effectively quenched the resulting yell of rage, and Dominic recovered his hold and kicked out powerfully for the distant sands.

For the first stage of that return journey, in the event more arduous and tedious than risky, he got no help from his passenger. But after a few minutes he was aware of a considerable skill seconding his own strokes; however sullenly, certainly to good effect. The kid had given up and resigned himself to being hauled ashore; and at least, having gone so far, he had sense enough to reason that he might as well make the journey as quickly and comfortably as possible. They came in like that, together, struggling steadily northward across the tug of the undertow into the sunny water off the beach, until they touched ground, and floundered wearily through the shallows, feet sliding deep into the soft, shaken sands.

Rising out of the water was an effort that sucked out their strength suddenly, and set them trembling and buckling at the joints with the realisation of their own tiredness. They fell together on their faces, toes still trailing in the receding foam, and lay gasping and coughing up sea-water. And there was the late afternoon sun on their backs, grateful and warm as a stroking hand, and the soft, almost silent waves lapping innocently on the long, level beach that stretched for more than two miles beyond Pentarno.

Dominic hoisted himself laboriously on his hands, and looked at his capture with something between a proprietor's pride and a keeper's exasperation. A slim, sunburned body, maybe fourteen or fifteen years old, in black swimming trunks. Light brown hair—probably almost flaxen when it was dry—streamed sea-water into the sand. He lay on his folded arms, the fine fan of his ribs clapping frantically for air, like cramped wings. Dominic got to his knees, hoisted the limp, light body by the middle, and squeezed out of him the remainder of the brine he had swallowed.

Hands and knees scrabbled in the sand, and the boy writhed away from him like an eel. Under the lank fall of hair one half-obscured eye, blue and steely as a dagger, glared fury.

"What the *hell*," spluttered the ungrateful child, from a mouth bitter with sea-water, "do you think you're—*doing*?" He choked and ran out of breath there. Dominic sat back on his heels and scowled back at him resentfully.

"Now, look here, you daft little devil, you'd do better thinking what the hell *you* were doing, out there in a sea like that. Don't you know the bathing's dead dangerous anywhere off the point? Especially when the tide's going out, like this. This town marks all the safe places, why can't you have the sense to stick to 'em? And don't give me that drop-dead look, either. You can thank your stars I was around. You'd have been in a mess without me."

"I would *not*! I wasn't in trouble——" He wavered for the first time; fundamentally he was, it seemed, a truthful person, even when in a rage. "I could have managed, anyhow. I know the tides round here a lot better than you do, I bet." The still indignant eyes had sized up a summer visitor without any difficulty. "Damn it, I *live* here."

"Then your dad ought to tan you," said Dominic grimly, "for taking such fool chances."

"I wasn't taking chances—not for nothing, I wasn't." He heaved a great breath into him, and swept back the fall of hair from his forehead. "I wouldn't—not without a good reason, my dad knows that. I went in because I saw a man in the sea——"

Dominic was on his feet in a flurry of sand. "You saw a *man*? You mean, somebody in trouble? Where?"

"Off the point, where I was, where d'you think? There was *something* being pulled out in the race, anyhow, I'm *nearly* sure it was a man. I swam out to try and get to him," said the boy, with bitter satisfaction in shifting the burden of his own frustration to more deserving shoulders, "but you had to take it on yourself to fish me out. So if he's drowned by now, you know whose fault it is, don't you?"

: :   : :

Dominic turned without a word, and set off at a run towards the water, his knees a little rubbery under him from shock and exertion. He had gone no more than a few yards when a shout from the dunes behind him brought him round again. The coast road from Maymouth over the neck of the Dragon's Head to Pentarno dipped closer to the beach here, and a man had just left it to drop in a series of leaps towards the sands. He had come from Maymouth, by the angle at which he appproached. A tall, agile, sudden man who could glissade down loose sand like a skier, and run, once he reached level ground, with the grace of a greyhound and the candour of a child. He came up to them full tilt, and checked in a couple of light steps, already reaching down to hoist the kneeling boy to his feet, examine him in one sweeping glance, and visibly sigh relief.

"Paddy, what's going on? Are you all right?" He turned

an abrupt smile upon Dominic. "What's he been up to? Did you have to haul him out, or something? But he can swim like a fish."

"I haven't been up to anything, Uncle Simon, honestly!" The injured voice grew shrill, and snapped off into a light, self-conscious baritone. Dominic had thought and hoped this might be the father, but even an uncle was very welcome, especially one as decisive as this.

Gratefully he blurted out what most needed saying : "He says he saw a man being dragged out to sea off the point. That's why he went so far out. But I was up on the path there, and I didn't see anyone except him. Maybe he'd have been all right—but I was afraid he might not. I thought I ought to fetch him in."

"You were very right, and I'm most grateful. Even if he isn't," said Uncle Simon with the briefest of grins. He stood Paddy before him firmly, and shook him by the shoulders. "Now, what did you see? Somebody throwing his arms about? Shouting for help? What?"

"No, he wasn't doing *anything* Not even, swimming. It was like a head just showing now and then, and there was more of it sort of sloshing about under the water— like when you see a drift of wood or some old rags washing about."

"It could have been just that, couldn't it?"

"Yes, I suppose so—only I don't think it was."

"O.K., I suppose we'd better have a hunt round." He stripped off his sportscoat and shirt, and dropped them beside the boy. "Here, you stay here and mind these."

"I'll come with you," said Dominic.

"Stay well inshore, then. And get out when you've had enough. I know this coast, you don't, and you've tired yourself already." He kicked his feet clear of his grey flannels. "Paddy, you can make yourself useful, too. Get up on the top path, and give us a hail if you see anything."

He was off down the beach and into the water, Dominic after him. Paddy's summer tan was only deep ivory compared with the tawny gold of Uncle Simon's long, mus-

cular back, and the fine, lean arms and legs that sliced
through the water without a ripple. His hair was not
more than a couple of shades darker. Once in the deep
water he swam like a dolphin. With unaccustomed humility
Dominic accepted his own lesser part, and forbore from
following too far. A man who could move with so much
confidence and certainty, off such a thorny coast, had the
right to deploy his forces as he thought best, and be
obeyed.

He stayed in the water until he felt himself tiring again,
and then he came out and made his way along the rocks
towards the Dragon's mouth, as low towards the sea as he
dared, watching Simon dive, and surface and dive again,
achingly near to the cauldron of the rocks. The worst of
the race was over now, the boiling had subsided a little.
The swimmer worked methodically outward along the
line of the receding tide, came back cautiously towards the
rocks again where the worst spite was already spent, and
clung to rest. He had torn his knuckles, Dominic saw
a pink ooze of blood on the hand that grasped the rock.

"No dice, Paddy?" he called up to the boy above their
heads.

"No, nothing." The voice shouted down a little gruffly
and anxiously: "You'd better come in, hadn't you?"
Even an Uncle Simon, presumably, may reach exhaustion
finally, and with him Paddy was taking no chances. "It's
no good now, anyhow. Even if it *was* somebody."

"All right—yes, I'll come."

He dropped carefully into the water and swam back to
the sand, preferring that to the slower climb along the
rocks. The boys came down, scrambling after him, Dominic
with his clothes bundled untidily under his arm.

The tall, tawny, sinewy man stood wringing water out
of his hair and streaming drops into the sand. Deep brown
eyes surveyed them as they came up, and he twitched a
shoulder and shivered a little. It was early September,
and the evenings were growing cool. They began to dress
in damp discomfort and a sudden chill of depression.

" No sign of anyone."

" Maybe there wasn't anyone," said Paddy grudgingly. "But honestly, I still think there was."

" All right, Paddy, you couldn't have done more, anyhow. I'll notify the coastguard, just in case, if that'll make you feel better. That's all we can do. What we all need now is a cup of tea, and some towels. And maybe a drop of rum in the tea. Come on up with us to the farm—Sorry, but what should I be calling you?"

" My name's Dominic Felse. We're staying at the Dragon."

" Well, Dominic, come on home with us, and get warm and dry. Can't let you run off now, without having thanked you properly."

Dominic hesitated, half afraid that this might more properly be the time for him to disappear, but deeply unwilling to do so if he could gracefully remain. At eighteen years and one week he held the optimistic view that you can never know too many people or accumulate too many friends; and the success of a holiday depends on what you find for yourself on the spot, not what you bring with you.

" Well—if I shan't be in the way? I mean—I don't think Paddy particularly wants to come home with a life-guard attached. Won't his people——?" It was a long time since he'd been Paddy's age, but with a heroic effort of the imagination he could still put himself in the other fellow's place.

" Now that's thoughtful of you, but take it from me, Dominic, this is one ego that needs no tenderness from you or anyone." He took Paddy by the nape of the neck and propelled him briskly towards the rising path that led up through the dunes towards the stubble-fields. " Come on, no argument!" He took Dominic, surprisingly but with absolute confidence, by the neck with the other hand, and hustled them into a trot. He was a man who could do things like that, and not only get away with it, but get himself liked for it, where someone less adept would have given electrifying offence.

"What about Paddy's clothes?"

"Oh, he came down from home in his trunks. Always does. First thing in the morning, and again in the afternoon. I told you, his parents gave birth to a herring. Come on, run for it!"

And they ran, glad to warm themselves with exercise; across the undulating coastal road, and through the hollow lane to the gate of Pentarno farm. A deep hollow of trees, startlingly lush and beautiful as always wherever there was shelter in this wild and sea-swept land, enfolded the solid grey stone house and the modern farm buildings.

"I don't live here," explained Simon as he opened the gate. "I'm just a long-standing nuisance from Tim's schooldays, that turns up from time to time and makes itself at home."

The front door stood open on a long, low, farmhouse hall, populous with doors. At the sound of their footsteps on the stone floor one of the doors flew open, and Philippa Rossall leaned out, in denims and a frilly pinafore, her arms flour to the elbow.

"Well, about time! I thought I should have to start 'phoning the hospitals. When you two quit showing up for *meals*——"

She broke off there, grey eyes opening wide, because there were not two of them, but three. She was middle-sized, and middling-pretty, and medium about everything, except that all the lines of her face were shaped for laughter. She had a mane of dark hair, and lop-sided eyebrows that gave her an amused look even in repose, and a smile that warmed the house.

"Oh, I didn't realise we had company. Hallo!" She took in suddenly their wet and tangled hair, and the way their clothes clung to them, and swung for an instant between astonishment and alarm, but beholding them all intact and apparently composed, rejected both in favour of amusement. "Well!" she said. "Never a dull moment with Simon Towne around. What have you all been doing? Diving off the pier for pennies? No, never mind, whatever you've been up to, go and get out of those clothes first, while I get my baking in and make another pot of tea. And be careful how you turn on the shower, the water's very hot. Simon, find him some of your clothes and take care of him, there's a lamb. Tim isn't in from the cows yet."

Tim came in at that moment by the back door, a large, broad, tranquil person with a sceptical face and guileless eyes, attired in a sloppy, hand-knitted sweater and corduroys.

"Bodies, actually," said Simon. "Off the point."

"Eh?" said Tim dubiously, brought up short against this cryptic pronouncement.

"Phil asked if we'd been diving for pennies off the pier. And I said, no, bodies. Off the point. But we didn't find any. This is Dominic Felse, by the way. Dominic's staying up at the Dragon. He was kind enough to fish Paddy out of the sea when he was in difficulties. Paddy says he wasn't in difficulties, but Dominic fished him out, anyhow. So we brought him back to tea."

"Good!" said Philippa, with such large acceptance that there was no guessing whether she meant to express gratification at having her offspring rescued from the Atlantic, or receiving an unexpected guest to tea. The look she gave Dominic was considerably more communicative, if he had not been too dazed to notice it.

"He fetched me a clip on the ear, too," volunteered Paddy, who would certainly not have mentioned this circumstance if he had not already forgiven it, and resolved to complete the removal of the smart by exorcism.

"Good!" said Tim. "Somebody should, every now and again. We're much obliged to you, Dominic. Stick around, if you enjoyed it—there may be other occasions."

The first, and brief, silence, which it must certainly have been Dominic's turn to fill, found him speechless, and drew all their eyes upon him in understanding sympathy. It appeared that the Rossall brand of verbal table-tennis had taken at a disadvantage this slender and serious young man who didn't yet know the rules.

"It's always this kind of a madhouse here," Paddy told

him kindly. "You'll get used to it. Just muck in and take everything for granted, it's the only way."

But it seemed that was not the trouble. Dominic had not even heard all the latter part of the conversation, and he did not hear this. He looked from Simon to Phil, and back to Simon again, and his eyes were shining.

"You did say *Simon Towne*? Really? You mean—*the* Simon Towne?"

"Heaven help us!" said Phil Rossall devoutly. "There surely can't be *two*?"

: :   : :

Dominic rushed up the stairs of the Dragon Hotel just after half-past seven, made a ten-minute business of changing, and tapped at his parents' door. Bunty, who had been struggling with the back zipper of her best dress, relaxed with a sigh of relief, and called him in.

"Just in time, darling! Come and do me up."

It was convenient to have him there at her shoulder, where she could watch him in the mirror without being herself watched, or observed to be watching. For the dark suit had surprised her. He was no fonder of dressing up, as a general rule, than his father. The look of restrained satisfaction which surveyed the sleek fit of the gold silk sheath over her shoulders, and the pleased pat he bestowed on her almost unconsciously as he closed the last inch of zipper, confirmed what the dark suit and the austere tie had suggested. Apparently she'd done the right thing. He was studying the total effect now with deep thoughtfulness. One more minute, and he'd have his fingers in her trinket-case, or be criticising her hair-style. Something was on for to-night; something she didn't yet know about. But by the mute, half-suppressed excitement of his face she soon would. Provided, of course, that she didn't ask.

"I was wondering where you'd got to. You must have walked a long way."

"Well, no, actually I never got very far. Something happened."

"Something nice?"

"Yes and no. Not really, I suppose. But then, I don't

think there ever was anyone there in the water, I think he just spotted some bit of flotsam. And then I had tea with some people I met." That had been nice, at any rate; he shone secretly at the remembrance, and with difficulty contained his own radiance. A girl? Bunty didn't think so, somehow. When remembering and containing encounters with girls he wore another face, conscientiously sophisticated and a little smug. This, though it strove after a man-of-the-world detachment, was the rapt face of a second-former noticed by the skipper of the First Fifteen.

He perched suddenly on the end of the dressing-table stool beside her, and put his arm round her, half to sustain his position, half in the old gambit that made confidences easy. The two faces, cheek to cheek in the mirror, were almost absurdly alike, oval, fair-complexioned, with freckled noses and large, bright hazel eyes. The two thick thatches of chestnut hair—She turned, nostrils quivering to the faint, damp scent, and put up a hand to feel at his forelock.

"Hmm! I see there was at least one someone there in the water. I didn't know you even took your trunks with you."

"I didn't, love! Look, I'll tell you!" But he'd do it his own way. He tightened his arm round her waist. The brightness was beginning to burst through. "Mummy, do you know who's staying in Maymouth?"

"Yes, darling, the distinguished Midshire C.I.D. man, Detective-Inspector George Felse, with his beautiful wife, and handsome and brilliant son." And the said George was already down in the bar, waiting for his family to join him for dinner; and the only concession he had made to the evening was to add a silk scarf to his open-necked shirt. Whereas it looked as if Dominic had everything lined up for a very special impression. She wondered if there'd be time to get George into a suit, and whether she owed it to Dominic to demand such a sacrifice of his father.

"Mummy, you said it! You look gorgeous. How about those black crystals? They'd go beautifully with this dress."

He had his fingers in among the few bits of finery she'd brought with her, fishing for the necklace he approved. " Keep still. No, but really, Mummy, do you know who's here? Not in the hotel, staying with some friends of his at the farm over at Pentarno. *Simon Towne* !"

She opened her eyes wide at the gleaming, triumphant face in the mirror. " No! Is he, *really*?" Now who on earth, she wondered for a moment, could Simon Towne be? This was a difficult game to play unless you had at least an inkling. Or, of course, there was always the deflationary play. The dead-pan face, the sudden flat, honest voice : " Who's Simon Towne?"

" Mummy, you shameless humbug! You were keener even than I was on those articles he did on Harappa and Mohenjo-daro. And that book on ancient and modern Peru—remember? Simon Towne is just about the most celebrated roving freelance journalist and broadcaster in the world, that's who Simon Towne is. As you very well know! And he's staying with the Rossalls at Pentarno until he sets off on another round-the-world commission in October. And I met him this afternoon!"

And I'm going to meet him to-night, thought Bunty with certainty; that's what all the fancy-work is for.

She took her exalted son by the arm and sat him firmly down beside her again. " You tell me every word about it, quickly."

He told her, and she paid him generously in reflected joy, and had no difficulty in appearing duly impressed; even *was* a little impressed. Yes, George would have to suffer; they couldn't let Dominic down. Meantime, she had to get downstairs ahead of him. It wasn't difficult; he'd given her enough clues.

" Sorry, Dom, I've mussed your hair a little. It's a bit fluffy from being wet so recently. Use George's cream. He left it in the bathroom, I think."

He went like a lamb. She called after him : " I'm going down, I'll be in the bar." And fled. He'd be five minutes re-settling his crest to his satisfaction.

George was on a stool at the bar, leaning on his elbow;

long and easy and thin, and physically rather elegant in his
heedless fashion, but not dressed for a momentous meeting.
Actually Bunty preferred him as he was, but a gesture
was called for.

She dug a hard little finger into his ribs from behind,
and said softly and rapidly into his ear : " Collar and tie
and suit, my boy, and hurry. Dom's captured a lion, and
I think he's bringing the whole pride in to coffee, or something."

George turned a face not yet shocked out of its comfortable languor. " Don't be funny, girl, it's nearly eight o'clock.
There isn't time. Even if I could be bribed to do it. I'm on
holiday, remember ?"

" So's Dom, and I tell you he's just aching to be proud
of us. Just once won't hurt you. Look at me !"

George did, and smiled. " You look good enough to
eat." He swivelled reluctantly on the stool. " Oh, all right,
I'll do it. But I won't perform."

" You won't get the chance, Dom will be straight man
to the lion, and the rest of us will be the audience. Go on,
quickly ! He's coming !"

George unfolded his long legs, looked at his watch, and
shot away in time to meet Dominic in the doorway. " Lord,
I've left it late to change. Got talking to Sam, and never
noticed the time. Go keep your mother company, I'll be
down in ten minutes."

Dominic, with a face of extreme maturity and dignity,
wound his way between the tables to the bar, and perched
himself without a word on the stool next to Bunty's. She
gave him a sweet, wide look which never wavered before
his severe stare. Behind the bar Sam Shubrough lifted
an interrogatory eyebrow.

" Manzanilla, please," said Dominic austerely, and slid
an uneasy hazel glance sideways at his mother. She hadn't
giggled; she hadn't made a sound or turned a hair, but
the effect was the same. He had been eighteen for such
a short time that he hadn't mastered his face yet on these
occasions.

" It's all right, lamb," she said in his ear wickedly,

" you're doing fine. You don't blush any more. But you haven't *quite* got over that tendency to a brazen stare yet."

" Thanks for the tip, I'll practise in front of a mirror. All right, Mum-Machiavelli," he said darkly. " You needn't think I don't know what a clever minx you are, because I do. Which tie did you tell him to put on?"

   : :   : :

" Anything you want to know about Maymouth and environs," said Tim Rossall, over coffee in the lounge, " just ask that well-known authority, Simon here. He's never been down here for more than three days at a time, not until this visit, but what he doesn't know about the place and its history by now isn't worth knowing. No, I mean it! He made a big hit with my Aunt Rachel, and she's given him the run of her library up there at the Place."

" The Place? That's Treverra Place? That big pile with the towers, at the top end of Maymouth?"

" That's it. Phoney towers, actually, they built 'em on late in the nineteenth century. The old girl rattles round in that huge dump like a pea in a drum, but she's still got the money to keep it up, and nobody else has. When she goes the National Trust will have to take it, or else it'll simply have to fall down."

" The National Trust wouldn't touch the place," said Phil cheerfully. " Tim's mother was Miss Rachel's younger sister. He's the last nephew, and he's horribly afraid she'll leave the house to him. There's a fine kitchen garden, though. She grows splendid apricots—a bit late ripening, but a lovely flavour. They'll be ready any day now, I must get her to send you some."

Dominic sat back happily in his corner and surveyed his successful and voluble party. They were all there but Paddy, who had gone to a cinema with friends of his own age; but Paddy, thought Dominic in the arrogance of his eighteen years, would have been bored, anyhow, in this adult circle. And they were getting on like a house afire. They'd liked one another on sight. Phil Rossall looked a different but equally attractive person with her dark hair coiled on top of her head, and her boy's figure disguised in a black, full-skirted dress. And Simon—no one ever seemed to call him anything but Simon—was the centre of any group he joined, even when he was silent and listening. Everything was going beautifully.

"A wild lot, these Treverras," Simon was saying, one wicked brown eye on Tim. "I'm thinking of writing the family history. Unless you make it worth my while not to, of course."

"Me? I'm relying on selling the film rights. Go right ahead. Two of 'em hanged for complicity in various faction plots, one time and another, several of 'em smuggled——"

"They *all* smuggled," said Phil firmly.

"But the most celebrated of the lot was the poet-squire, Jan Treverra, in the eighteenth century. Go on, Simon, you're the expert, tell 'em about Jan."

"On your own head be it! No one can stop me once I start. But let's adjourn to the bar, shall we? It's cosier down there."

They adjourned to the bar. There was a panelled corner that just held them all, with one place to spare, and Phil spread her skirt across that, with the glint of a smile at Simon.

"That's for Tam, if she drops in later."

"Tam?"

"Tamsin Holt, Aunt Rachel's secretary. It's only a quarter of an hour's walk from the Place, across the Dragon's neck. We're about on the same level, up here. And I should think the poor girl's had enough of Miss Rachel by evening. She is," said Phil blandly, "the real reason for Simon's passionate interest in the Treverra Library. She's re-cataloguing it and collating all the family papers. And when she takes off her glasses she isn't bad-looking. All right, Simon, go ahead, give us the story of Jan Treverra."

Simon lay back in his corner and talked. Not expertly, not with calculation, it was better than that; halting sometimes, relapsing into his own thoughts, hunting a word and coming up with it thoughtfully and with pleasure, as if it had a taste. Some of his writing was like that, the lamest and the most memorable. Dominic had the impression that those particular pages had been born out of his less happy moments.

" Jan was an individualist who smuggled and wrote and hunted in these parts about the middle of the eighteenth century. You must have noticed St. Nectan's church, I suppose? You'll have read about it even before you came here, if you're the kind of person who does read a place up before he visits it?"

"We read about it," admitted George. "We're the kind."

"Good, I like that kind. Then you know all about it, and anyhow you can see it from the top windows here. Over in the dunes, where they've been planting all the tamarisks to try and stop the sand marching inland. I don't know exactly what it is about this north coast, but there are several of these areas of encroaching sand, and nearly all of 'em have churches amidships to get buried. It's never houses, always churches."

"They're surely digging out St. Nectan's, aren't they?" George looked across at Bunty. "You remember, they'd uncovered all the graveyard when we were over there, and that's several days ago."

"*We're* digging it out. With these two hands I've shovelled sand to get at what I want. The fact is, as Tim will tell you, they do get fits of conscience here every now and again, and dig the place out, but they always forget it again as soon as they've finished, and in a couple of months the sand's got it again. But the point is, that's where Jan Treverra's buried. He had a massive tomb dug out for himself there before he was fifty, right down into the rock, and he wrote his own epitaph, ready for when he died. He even wrote one for his wife, too. In verse. Not his best verse, but not bad, at that. And soon after he was fifty he did die, of a fever, so they say. Quite a character was Jan. His life was not exemplary, but at least it had gusto, and it was never mean. He was a faithful husband and a loyal friend. The whole district idolised him, and his wife pined away within six months of his death, and joined him in his famous vault. His poems were pretty good, actually. There's a tradition that some of them were buried with him, at his own orders, and now Miss Rachel's developed a desire to find out if it's true."

"Not unprompted," said Phil, "by Simon. Any quest that gives him free access to the library will have our Simon's enthusiastic support. As long as Tamsin's in there, of course."

"Not that it's getting me anywhere," admitted Simon with a charmingly rueful smile. "She's refused me eight times, so far. Funny, she doesn't seem to take me seriously. Where was I? Oh, yes. On the night following Mrs. Treverra's funeral there was a sudden violent storm. It drove all the fishing boats out to sea, and wrecked two of them. And young Squire Treverra, the new owner, was out walking by himself on the cliff path when the wind suddenly rose, and he was blown off into the sea and drowned. They never recovered his body. So there never was another burial in the old vault, because by the time the younger brother died it was past 1830, and they'd given up the struggle with the sand, and built St. Mary Magdalene's, right at the top end of Maymouth. They didn't intend to lose *that* one. So for all we know it may be true about the poems in the coffin. Anyhow, as Maymouth's in the throes of its periodical fit of conscience about letting St. Nectan's get silted up, we're in a fair way to find out."

"You're thinking of opening the tomb?" asked George with interest.

"We've got a dispensation. In the interests of literature. If we miss this chance, who knows when we shall get another?" He thumped a fist suddenly and peremptorily on the oak table. "And I propose—Hear ye! Hear ye!—I propose to do the job the day after to-morrow, as ever is."

The whole public bar heard it, and several heads turned to grin in their direction; there was nobody among the Dragon's regulars whom Simon did not know, or who did not know Simon. Sam Shubrough heard it, and beamed broadly over the glass he was polishing. And the girl just entering the bar by the outside door heard it, and turned towards them at a light, swinging walk, her hands in the pockets of her fisher-knit jacket.

"Hallo!" she said, over Dominic's startled shoulder. "What's Simon advertising? Carpet sale, or something?"

"Tamsin!" The men shuffled to find foot-room to rise, and Phil drew her skirt close and made room for the newcomer in the circle.

"One thing about a man who announces his intentions through a megaphone," she said as she sat down and stretched out her long and very graceful legs, "you do at least know where he is, and how to avoid him."

"You came straight here, a pin to a magnet," said Simon promptly.

She looked round the table and counted. "There are six of you here. Five would have been enough. Some," she added, with a smile of candid interest that robbed her directness of all offence, "I don't know yet. I'm Tamsin Holt."

Tim did the honours. She smiled last and longest at Dominic, because he was looking at her with such startled and appreciative eyes. "Hallo! Phil told me about you. You pulled her Patrick out of the water this afternoon."

"Did she tell you he didn't want to come?" Dominic felt his colour rising; but the tide of pleasure in him rose with it. She was so astonishing, after Phil's mendacious description. Glasses, indeed! The bridge of her straight nose had certainly never carried any such burden. And as for "not bad-looking"!

"She told me maybe he didn't even *need* to come. But she said she'd like to think there'd always be you around whenever he even *might* need you. Take it from me, my boy, you're in. You've been issued with a membership ticket." She looked up over her shoulder, where Sam Shubrough's granite bulk was looming like one of the Maymouth rocks, a monolith with a good-humoured beetroot for a face. Half of its royal redness was concealed behind a set of whiskers which looked early-nineteenth-century-coachman, but were actually ex-R.A.F., "Hallo, Sam! Nice night for a walk."

To judge by the small, demure glint that flashed from her eyes to the landlord's, this meant more than it said. But then, she had a way of making everything a fraction more significant. Ever since she had sat down beside him Dominic had been trying to assimilate the complete image of her, and she wouldn't give him the chance. She was always in motion, and all he could master was the lovely detail.

"That right, now," asked Sam interestedly, peering down at Dominic from behind the hedge, "that you fetched young Paddy out? That's the first time anybody's ever had to do *that*. Where'd he manage to get into trouble?"

"Off the rocks of the point, just in the ebb, the worst time."

"Go on! What possessed a bright kid like him to go out there? He knows a lot better than that."

"He thought he saw a body being pulled out to sea there," Dominic explained. "He went in to try and reach him. But we went in afterwards and hunted as long as we could—at least, Mr. Towne did, I didn't do much—and there wasn't a sign of anything."

"A body, eh! Not that it would be the first time, by many a one. But I've heard no word of anyone being missing, or of anything being sighted. No boat's been in trouble for months, this is the best of the season. You reckon there's anything in it, Simon?"

"I doubt it," said Simon tranquilly. "He saw something, he's no fool. But I don't think for a moment it was a man. Bit of driftwood, or something, even a cluster of weed, that'll be all."

"Well," said Sam comfortably, accumulating empty glasses with large, deft fingers, "if it was a body, we'll probably know by to-morrow. Way the wind's setting now, the next incoming tide in the small hours will leave it high and dry on the Mortuary, same as it always does."

"The Mortuary?" Simon looked up with raised brows.

"That stretch of sand this side the church at Pentarno, where all the weed builds up. Almost anything that goes out off the point comes in again next tide on that reach.

Many a one we've brought in from there. They don't call it the Mortuary for nothing." He stood brandishing his bouquet of dead men, and beamed at them cheerfully. "What'll it be, Miss Holt? Gin and tonic? Any more orders, ladies and gents?"

George claimed the round, and Dominic backed carefully and gracefully out of it, because both his mother and his father had refrained from looking at him as if he ought to.

Something remarkable had happened suddenly to the circle. The two vehement people, the two who glittered and were always in motion, had fallen still and silent together. Simon was sitting with his hands folded before him on the table, all the lines of his long-boned face arrested in a Gothic mask, the brightness of his eyes turned inward. The stillness of the energetic often has a quite unjustified effect of remoteness and sadness. Their sleep sometimes has a look of withdrawal and death. And Tamsin—Dominic could see her whole for the first time, the pale oval of her face, the broad, determined brow under the smooth fringe of red-gold hair, the thoughtful, fierce and tender mouth, a little too large for perfection but just the right size for generosity and beauty; and the eyes, very dark blue under their startling black lashes, wide and watchful and withholding judgment, fixed upon Simon. If he looked at her she would lower the more steely blue of the portcullis, and her mouth would shape a dart quickly and hurl it. But now she studied, and thought, and wondered, and could not be sure.

"Gin and tonic," said Sam, leaning between them with the tray. "Bitter? Whisky on the rocks, that's Simon. Mild—that's Mr. Felse."

Simon came out of his abstraction with a start, and reached for his whisky.

"Doing the job down at the church day after tomorrow, are you?" said Sam conversationally. "That'll be a day for Maymouth. Nobody still kicking about it being irreverent, and all that?"

It was rather quiet in the bar. A frieze of benign local

faces beamed at the corner table. A tenuous little cord of private fun drew them all close together for a moment.

"Only the cranks, Sam, only the cranks. Look at the topweight we've got on our side. The church sanctions it, and Miss Rachel insists on it. Tim will represent the family's interests, and the Vicar'll be there to see fair play. How about you, Sam? Come and make a fourth witness? Ten o'clock in the morning, sharp!"

Just for a fraction of a second those two looked each other blandly in the eye, and the Maymouth regulars grinned like gargoyles along the wall.

"Wouldn't miss it, Simon," said Sam Shubrough heartily. "Any time you want a strong-arm man, you call on me. Ten o'clock sharp. I'll be there."

::   ::

From the hotel on the headland a broad path brought them to the slight dip of the Dragon's neck, where the road between Maymouth and Pentarno clambered over the hump-backed beast that slept in the moonlight. Their path crossed it and moved on through the highest roads, half back-street, half country-lane, of the quiet town of Maymouth, towards the towered monstrosity of Treverra Place.

"It's a lovely night," said Dominic dreamily, halting at the edge of the road, unwilling to cross, and shorten the way he still had to walk beside her.

"Lovely," said Tamsin.

"If you're not tired——"

"I'm not tired."

"I thought we could walk along the cliff road towards Pentarno a little way, and then turn in by the other lane."

"If you like, yes, of course."

It was his day. She'd said yes to everything he'd suggested, the first dance, the offer to escort her home, and now this delicate prolonging of his pleasure. Perhaps to leave him room to expand and show his paces, because that was what he wanted, and she liked him well enough to give him his head, and certainly needed no help to manage him. Or perhaps to mark more clearly how firmly she had said no to everything Simon had asked of her. She had played Dominic's game neatly back to him, and she knew already what he didn't yet know: that he wasn't in love with her in the least degree, and never would be, though there would be times when he would feel that he was. Nobody was going to get hurt by the game, it wasn't going to get rough; but they would both enjoy it and learn something from it, and be a little bit the richer ever after. What she hadn't expected was that he would say anything in the least extraordinary or out of the pattern. And when he had, their relationship had opened out on quite another plane. The game would delight him while his holiday lasted, and make it memorable afterwards. But the second relationship might well last much longer, and be seriously valued by them both. And neither of them would break any hearts. So she went on saying yes; yes to everything.

They had reached the edge of the dunes, and halted there on the seaward side of the road. The moon laid rippling scallops of luminosity along the sea, and away on their right the squat spire of St. Nectan's tiny church protruded from its hollow of sand, half-obscured by the ruled hedges of tamarisks.

" Tamsin—may I call you Tamsin?"

"Yes, of course, Dominic."

"Tamsin—how much do you really like Simon?"

She had never been more startled in her life. It hadn't taken her long to see that he was almost as dazzled by Simon as Paddy himself. She couldn't blame him; she knew all about that powerful magnetism, even if she herself was immune from responding to it. But he wasn't protesting or wondering, he was asking her, as one friend to another. Maybe he felt it flattering to be even a make-believe rival of the great man. Or maybe he just wanted to know. Or maybe, even more dangerously, he wanted to hear what she would say, because she wouldn't be answering him, and that would tell him a great deal.

"I like him well enough, but for certain attitudes. And those I don't like at all."

"Then he really has asked you to marry him?"

At first she thought that his sophistication must have slipped very badly to permit him to ask such a thing; then the deliberation of his voice warned her that they were on the second plane, and this was in earnest.

"Yes, he has."

"Eight times?"

"I haven't counted. Probably. Most times we meet."

"Why don't you?"

"Why don't I what? Count?"

"Marry him."

"Look," she said, turning her back on the shining innocence of the sea, "even if he meant it, the answer would still be no. But he doesn't. He's spoiled and flippant and mischievous, and in bad need of a fall. He's only had to smile at people all his life, and whatever he wanted has fallen into his lap. And he doesn't care what he breaks in the process. No, that's too steep. He just doesn't realise that he breaks anything, all he sees is his own wants. He's just having fun with me."

"*I* shouldn't think it much fun," said Dominic, "to ask you to marry me and get turned down."

"You're not Simon, my dear. Do you think he'd be concerning himself with why I turned *you* down—supposing I ever did?"

"No," agreed Dominic honestly, "but then, he's in love with you, and——"

It was the first mistake he had made, fumbling between the two planes of his liking for her, and he was thrown out of his stride by the gaffe. To cover himself he took her rather agitatedly in his arms, gingerly in case she objected, but already almost persuaded she wouldn't. She was laughing; she shook gently with honest amusement against his chest.

"And you're not! Go on, say——"

He did not so much lose his head as throw it away, and without it he was much more adept. He felt gently downward with his lips to her mouth, and kissed her. It wasn't the first time, he knew what he was doing. But perhaps it was the first of its kind, warm and impulsive and affectionate, and quite untroubled.

When it was over he held her for some minutes still, not wanting to talk.

"That wasn't necessary," she said in his ear.

"No, I know it wasn't."

"Aren't you going to say you're sorry?"

"No. I'm glad. I enjoyed it very much, and so did you. But I won't do it again, because it would spoil it."

"You," she said helplessly, "are an extraordinary boy."

"I wouldn't be, if I were with an ordinary girl."

His cheek against hers, the baffling unusualness of the day overwhelming him with the delicious conviction of complete happiness, suddenly he froze. His mind went away from her, somewhere there over her shoulder, down among the dunes. She pushed him away suddenly, and turned to look.

"Tamsin, do you see what I see? Look, there between the tamarisks." One man, two, three, slipping along out of the landward hollow, keeping in the tenuous shade of the young hedges, moving towards the church in its deep nest.

Tamsin shivered and took his arm, turning him about and drawing him landward across the road. "Ugh, it's getting cold. I'd better get home, Dominic. Come on, we've got ten minutes' walking yet."

::   ::

George was still on the hotel terrace, smoking his last pipe and watching the sea.

"Hallo!" he said, hearing the unmistakable step of his son and heir moving up on him quietly from the garden. "How'd you make out?"

"Don't be nosy," said Dominic austerely, and came and sat down on the arm of the chair.

"Dad——"

"Hmmm?"

"Do you suppose," asked Dominic very casually, "that there's much smuggling in these parts nowadays?"

After a long and cautious silence George said weightily :
"Now, look, I'm on holiday. I intend to remain that way.
The local excisemen and police are quite capable of running
their own show. And it's no business of mine where Sam
gets his brandy."

"That's what I thought," said Dominic cheerfully. "So,
quite unofficially, of course, what d'you make of this?"
And he told him exactly what he had seen in the region
of St. Nectan's church, though not the precise circumstances
in which he had come to see it.

"Going towards the church," said George carefully.
"And Tamsin took good care to remove you from the
vicinity as soon as she realised what was going on. Yes,
quite interesting."

"Especially," said Dominic, "since Simon made such
a point of broadcasting in the bar exactly when he intended
to open the Treverra vault. And then grinned at Sam,
and invited him——"

"Or dared him?" suggested George.

"——to be present on the occasion. And the hint and the
challenge were taken. On the spot."

"Now I wonder just where the safe-deposit was?"

"I wonder, too. In the vault itself, do you think?"

"Now mind," said George warningly, "not a word to
anyone else. We're only in this game by courtesy, if we're
in it at all. It's the local man's manor."

Dominic rose from the arm of the chair, and stretched
and yawned magnificently.

"What do you take me for?" he said scornfully, and
strolled away to bed.

CHAPTER II

THURSDAY

" It's to-morrow, then," observed Paddy, coming in damp and boisterous from his morning swim, and plumping himself down hungrily at the breakfast table.

Tim looked up from the paper. " What's to-morrow?"

" The big day. The day we take the lid off the old gentleman. Mummy said Uncle Simon was alerting the squad last night. Wouldn't do if anybody got caught with his pants down, would it? Except the squire, I suppose it's all one to him by this time."

Not at his most gay and extrovert in the morning, Tim squinted almost morosely at his son over his coffee cup, and wondered if anyone, even at fifteen, could really be as bright and callous as this before breakfast.

" I know!" said Paddy, fending off the look with a grin. " That's no way to talk about the dead. Still, I bet he's the only one around Maymouth who isn't excited about this bit of research. *I* am! And if you're not, you ought to be. It's your family. And just think, we may be making history." He reached for the cereal packet as if it had been the crock of gold, and helped himself liberally. " Mummy, how's that fresh coffee coming?"

From the corridor Phil's voice retorted hollowly : " Being carried by me, as usual." She came in with the tray, and closed the door expertly with her elbow.

Paddy received his cup, laced it with brown sugar to his liking, and returned happily to h:s preoccupation.

" Think we really shall find anything, Dad? In the coffin?"

Phil stiffened, the coffee-pot suspended in her hand. She looked from her husband to her son, and inquired in suspiciously mild tones : " And where did you get the 'we'?"

Paddy's eyes widened in momentary doubt and dismay,

and smiled again in the immediate confidence that she must be pulling his leg. "Come off it! You wouldn't go and spoil it, would you? Not when it's Uncle Simon's own personal project? I've got to be there, of course." His smile sagged a little; her face hadn't melted. "Oh, gosh, you *wouldn't* make me miss the only bit of real excitement there's ever going to be in Maymouth?" Inevitably he appealed to Tim across the table. "Dad, you didn't say I couldn't. We were just talking about it, and you *didn't* say——"

"I didn't say you could," said Tim, truthfully, but aware that he was hedging. He looked doubtfully at Phil's cloudy face, observed the set of her jaw, and could have kicked himself. He should have known that she wouldn't think grubbing about among tombs and bones a proper occupation for her ewe lamb. Mothers are like that. Especially mothers as achingly unsure of their hold on what they love as Phil.

"No, but I thought you understood that I was taking it for granted. You must have known I wanted to be there, you could have told me right away if you didn't mean to let me. I'm sorry if I should have asked, but I never thought. I'll ask now. Please, Mummy, is it all right with you if I go along with Uncle Simon and Dad to open Jan Treverra's tomb to-morrow?"

He recited this in a parody of his child's voice, wrinkling his nose at her provocatively; which, according to all the rules, should have been the right thing, and paid off handsomely. But it wasn't the right thing, and it wasn't going to pay off. He saw it at once, and was appalled to think he had so stupidly clinched the case against himself. Never reduce anything to a formula; if you do, you're stuck with it.

"No," said Phil, gently but firmly, "I'm sorry, but it isn't all right with me. You're not going, and that's that. Now forget it."

Paddy pushed his chair back a little, brows drawn down over a level and injured stare. "Why not? Why don't you want me to?"

"Because it's no place for you, and I'd rather you stayed away from it."

"Think I'd be having nightmares?" he demanded, suddenly breaking into a broad but uncertain smile. "Now, look, Mummy, I'm fifteen. I know what bones are like, and I know we're all going the same way in the end. It doesn't worry me a bit. You needn't be afraid I'll turn morbid."

"*No!*" said Phil with unmistakable finality, refusing argument. She herself couldn't be certain of her motives, but she knew that the thought of letting him go down those sand-worn steps into the vault horrified her, and at all costs she wanted to prevent it.

Paddy recognised a closed and locked door, but would not acknowledge it as impassable. He made the mistake of casting a glance sidelong at Simon's place, where a carelessly folded newspaper left lying showed the state of the day. Apparently he'd breakfasted already, which was unusual and a pity. He could have diverted this disaster if it had threatened in his presence. Paddy pushed away his plate, and smoothed his forehead conscientiously, like a man-of-the-world tactfully recognising when to change the subject.

"Where's Uncle Simon?"

"No good," said Tim, not without sympathy. "You haven't an ally, my boy. He's gone up to the Place already."

"Up early, wasn't he?" The implication that he was looking round for support he ignored, though he knew nobody was deceived.

"Now, look, Paddy," said Tim with emphasis, "let it alone. She's said no, and I say no, and that's all about it."

Paddy's fist slammed the table. He jerked his chair back and was on his feet in a blaze of rage. That temper had cost them plenty in patience and forbearance in his early years, but they hadn't seen much of it lately, and this abrupt flare was as startling as lightning. It was almost a man's rage, quiet and quivering. The dilated nostrils looked almost blue with tension.

"What are you trying to do, keep me a kid? You can't!

If I've got to grow up in spite of you, I'll do it that way, and be damned to it!"

He didn't even shout; his voice was lower than usual. And he turned and flung out of the room and out of the house before either of them could draw breath to stop him.

: :   : :

"The awful part of it is," owned Phil, "I don't know how honest I'm being about this. I don't want him to go, I don't think it's any place for an adolescent boy. But I know darned well I'm jealous of Simon. He only has to crook his finger, and Paddy comes running. You'd think no one else existed, this last week or so. It scares me."

"Our own fault, I suppose." Tim turned glumly from the window and looked her in the eyes long and sombrely. "We ought to have known we should have to tell him, sooner or later. We should have done it long ago. I only wish we had."

"But how could we know we should have to? I know it's supposed to be bad policy not to. But we were going to move here, everything was new. Nobody knew us, except Aunt Rachel. Nobody cared. I couldn't see any *reason*. And now—how in the world could we ever set about it, after all this time?"

"We couldn't. We daren't. There isn't a thing we can do, except just keep our fingers crossed, and let him alone. It won't be long now."

"No," she agreed, but only half-comforted. "Tim—suppose Simon tells him?"

"No! He wouldn't do that. He's always kept his bargain so far, hasn't he?"

"He's never really wanted to break it before," said Phil cynically, "but this time he does. And much as I like him, I wouldn't trust him far when he's after something he wants."

She got up with a sigh, and began loading the breakfast dishes on to the tray. There had been a time when she had been equally jealous of Simon's influence over Tim, until she found out by experience that Tim, after his quiet fashion, went his own way, and was very unlikely to be deflected from it by Simon or anyone else.

"Think I'd better go after him?"

"Tim, don't you dare give way to him, after I've gone and committed myself!"

"You've committed me, too," said Tim with a wry grin. "Don't worry—united we stand! Still, it was pretty much my fault he'd got the programme all set up like that. I think I'd better go and find him, and get him cooled down."

But Paddy was not in the house, or the garden, or the yard, nor was he visible anywhere on the road to the sea. Tim came back empty-handed.

"His bike's gone from the shed. Never mind him, let him go. He'll be back for his lunch. Give him that, at any rate, he doesn't sulk for long."

"What'll you bet," said Phil sharply, "he hasn't gone rushing up to the Place after Simon? I *bet* you! He thinks Simon will get round us. He thinks Simon can get round anybody."

She plunged upon the telephone in the hall, and dialled the number of Treverra Place.

"Oh, hallo, Tam——"

But it wasn't Tamsin; the telephone was switched to Miss Rachel's room, and the old lady was wide awake and only too ready to talk. And perhaps that was better, for if it had been Tamsin and the library, more than likely Simon would have been there to hear one half of the conversation and deduce the other.

"Oh, it's you, Aunt Rachel. This is Phil. Listen, is Simon there in the library right now? No, I don't want him, I just want to know. Good, that's fine. Well, look, if our Paddy comes looking for him, don't tell him where he's gone, will you? And don't let Tamsin tell him. I know he'll find him in the end, but he won't think of the vicarage for a while, anyhow—long enough for him to think better of it, I hope."

"Exactly why," inquired Miss Rachel curiously, "should he be on his way here, and why don't you want him to find

Simon? Oh, I'll do what you say, naturally. But I do like to have reasons for what I'm doing."

Phil sat down and drew the instrument into a comfortable position for a long session. Tim, recognising the signs, sighed and left them to it. What could you do with women? They were as dead set on not being outwitted or defeated as the kid himself, but it wouldn't be any use pointing out the illogic of their proceedings; they'd never be able to see the analogy.

::   ::

By the time Paddy had pedalled furiously up the sunken lane and was breasting the climb into the outskirts of Maymouth, he had worked most of the spite out of him, and was coming to the conclusion that after all there was something to be said for his parents' point of view. Not much, of course, but something. Maybe, after all, he wouldn't go behind their backs and coax or trick Simon into promising him what they had denied. For pure pleasure he kept telling himself that he would, but the sight of the absurdly tall and ponderous gateposts of Treverra Place forced him to slow his pace and make up his mind. He took the long drive in a weaving course from rhododendrons to rhododendrons, like a contestant in a slow-bike race, fighting it out. He would, he wouldn't. He wouldn't! He was fifteen, not a spoiled kid in a tantrum. He'd go back at lunch-time, and apologise.

Still, now that he was here he might as well drop in and say hallo to Miss Rachel and Tamsin. In fact, he'd have to, because one of them had spotted him already.

Miss Rachel was parading the stretch of gravel in front of the embattled Victorian front door, upright and stocky in a gaudy tweed skirt and hand-knitted purple jumper, the image of an elderly country gentlewoman from a distance. At close quarters she was more of a stage version of the same character, with a mobile, actress's face and bold, autocratic gaze, with a sort of instability about the whole impersonation, as if she was only waiting to complete her scene before whipping off the make-up and dressing for quite another role in quite another play. The one thing that didn't change was that she must always be the central personage. Sometimes she reminded Paddy of Queen Victoria, because of her imperious and impervious respectability and her general shape; at other times he thought of her as a local and latter-day Queen Elizabeth, because she had so successfully charmed younger men after her through most of her life, and could do so still when she really tried. Probably she had stayed single to keep her power, like her great prototype before her, though not for such grand and statesmanlike ends, but for her own personal pleasure.

He was very fond of her. She told him off and complained of him very often, but he didn't have to be a genius to know that she adored him, and that was nearly enough to ensure his affection in return. What clinched it was the unexpected amount of fun she could be at times, sometimes even his ally against the generation in between. She was all the grandmother he had, and grandmothers are a reassuring article of equipment in any boy's life.

So when he saw her stumping up and down examining her roses, it was natural enough to him to turn his bicycle from the main drive along the intricate paths between the flower-beds, and ride down upon her in a sudden flurry of fine gravel, circling her three or four times before he put a foot to the ground and halted to face her. He was at peace with himself by that time, and his face was sunny. They'd been stuffy, but he'd been a complete oaf. He wouldn't do a thing to widen the breach; he'd make his peace like a lamb as soon as he went home.

"Hallo!" he said, uncoiling himself at leisure from the bike and propping it against the huge scraper by the front steps. "You'm looking very peart this morning, me dear."

"Am I, indeed?" She tapped her stick peremptorily on the stones that bordered the rose-bed, and gave him a narrowed and glittering glance of her still handsome black eyes. "Buttering me up will get you nowhere, my boy, let me tell you that for a start. I'm wise to you. You didn't come all the way up here to see me, did you? Oh, dear, no!"

"Well, for Pete's sake!" said Paddy blankly. "What

have I done to you this morning? Did you get out of bed the wrong side? I've only just set foot in the place, give me a chance."

"Oh, I know! Innocence is your middle name. But it's no use, young man, you're wasting your time. You won't find Simon in the library. He isn't here. And Tamsin won't tell you where he is, either."

"I wasn't going to——" he began, stung and enlightened by this attack; and there, remembering in what a state of indecision he had arrived at the gate, he halted and flushed in guilty indignation.

"Oh, no, not *you*! You wouldn't dream of running to Simon behind your mother's back, would you? Don't think I don't know what was in your mind. You think he'll be able to twist your parents round his finger, and get you everything you want, don't you? Even when they've said no. Yes, you see, I know all about it."

Yes, he saw, and he saw exactly how she had learned what she knew. It didn't take much imagination to reconstruct. His mother must have been on the line like a tigress. What galled him most deeply was not that she should be so determined to frustrate him, but that she should be able to see through him as through plate glass, and anticipate his moves so accurately. And he'd won his struggle and come to terms with her in his mind before it ever came to the point of action. But she'd never made a move towards reconciliation in *her* mind, never allowed for the possibility that he might relent and think better of it. Who was going behind whose back?

"Patrick, you're not listening to me!" The old lady was half-way through the expected lecture, and he hadn't heard a word.

"I am listening," he said, with bewildering meekness, only half his mind present, the meek half. The rest, hurt, vengeful and obstinate, ranged bitterly after his mother's treason. If she wanted that sort of fight, if she could immediately accept battle on those terms, and never give him the benefit of the doubt, well, she could have it that way.

"If they've said no, that should be enough for you. You're not a little boy now, you know enough to realise they have your best interests at heart, and I thought you had sense enough to accept their judgment, even where you couldn't quite agree with it. Fancy losing your temper over a little thing like that! I'm ashamed of you!"

So his mother hadn't even kept *that* quiet. What could you do with women? They were all the same.

"I was ashamed of myself," he said, with unexampled mildness; which pleased Miss Rachel so much that she never noticed the significance of the tense he had used. So he had been ashamed, for a few chastened and happy moments as he slow-biked up the drive. But not any more.

"That's better. I know you're not a bad boy at heart. Now you're to put it right out of your mind, you hear me? They've said no, and that's to be the end of it. You're not to pester Simon. You'll go right home and tell your mother you're sorry."

Will I, hell! thought Paddy very succinctly. Aloud he said: "O.K., I'm on my way, Aunt Rachel." But he took good care not to say where.

She watched him mount his bike with exaggerated solemnity, salute her gravely, and pedal away down the drive again in a caricature of penitence and self-examination. He wasn't even ashamed of pulling her leg. Practically speaking, she wasn't in the act at all, she was just a miscalculation on his mother's part.

And now, since that was the way his mother wanted it, now he *would* find Simon, if it took him all day.

: :   : :

It didn't take him all day, but it did take him all morning. He'd tried the church in the sands, and the church in the town, and several other places, before he ran Simon to earth at noon in the lounge of the Dragon, snug in a corner between George and Dominic Felse, with three halves of bitter on their table. Paddy hesitated for a moment, somewhat daunted at having to prefer his plea before witnesses; but in the instant when he might have drawn back, Simon turned his head and saw him hovering.

"Hallo, there!" There was no doubting the welcome and pleasure in his face, but wasn't he, all the same, a shade sombre this morning, a Simon faintly clouded over? To-morrow was, Paddy reminded himself with a start of surprise and a slight convulsion of an uneasy conscience, a very serious business. "Looking for me? Anything the matter?" They made room for him, all three re-arranging their chairs; he was in it now, he couldn't back out.

"No, nothing. I just wanted—But I'm afraid I'm interrupting you."

"Not in the least. Oh, I forgot you two hadn't met before. This is Paddy Rossall, George. Say good-morning to Dominic's father, Paddy."

He had got something out of his pursuit, at any rate. He fixed George with large and hungry eyes. Did he look like a detective-inspector? The trick, he supposed, was not to look like one, but at least George Felse would do pretty well. Tall and thin, with a lean, thoughtful face and hair greying at the temples; not bad-looking, in a pleasant, irregular way. Paddy paid his respects almost reverently, and accepted the offer of a ginger ale.

"What did you want to ask me?"

"Well—if it's all right with you, could I come along and help you to-morrow?" It was out, and in quite a creditable tone, though he had the hardest work in the world not to embroider it with all manner of persuasions and coaxings. His conscience suffered one more convulsive struggle before he suppressed it. If he hadn't confessed that his parents had already forbidden it, still he hadn't told any lies. It was a matter of his adult honour, by this time, not to admit defeat.

Simon sat looking at him for a few moments with an unreadable face, almost as though his mind had wandered away to ponder other and less pleasant subjects. "It's like this, Paddy," he said at last, almost abruptly. "I can't very well say yes to you, in fairness, because I've just said no to Dominic here. There are good reasons, you know. Space is short inside there. And then, this isn't an entertainment, you see, it's a bit of serious research. It wouldn't be the thing to turn it into a spectacle. The witnesses are necessary for the record, not for their own satisfaction."

In the few seconds of silence George and Dominic exchanged a brief, significant glance over Paddy's averted head. The boy studied his ginger ale as though the secret of the universe lay quivering somewhere in the globule of amber light suspended in it. His face was a little too still to be quite convincing, though the air of commonsense acceptance with which he finally looked up could be counted a success.

"Well, that all makes sense. O.K., then, that's it. You didn't mind my asking, though?"

"Paddy, in other circumstances I don't know a fellow anywhere I'd rather have to help me."

"Thanks! I'll remember that. I suppose I'd better be getting back to lunch, then. You won't be coming?"

"No, I'm lunching here. I told your mother this morning."

"Well, thanks for the drink." He tilted the empty glass and slanted a quick smile up at George. "Good thing it was only ginger ale." He rose, his face still a little wry with swallowing his disappointment.

"Why, in particular?" asked Simon curiously.

The boy divided a bright, questioning glance between them. "Didn't you really know? You've got a real, live detective-inspector sitting right beside you, watching your every move. Mr. Felse would have pinched you in a flash if you'd stood me a shandy." He waved a hand, not ungallantly. "Good-bye!" He was gone.

"Well, I'm damned!" said Simon, blankly staring. "Are you really?"

George admitted it. "But I don't know how Paddy found out."

"I told him," said Dominic, a little pink with embarrassment at seeming still, at his mature age, to be boasting about his father's profession. "When he walked back half-way here with me yesterday, after tea at the farm. We hadn't exactly got off on the right foot with each other, I was rather casting about for acceptable lures. There was Simon

———" He smiled rather self-consciously across the table at the great man. "Anyone who knows your Harappa articles almost by heart is practically in with Paddy. And the next bid seemed to be you, Dad. He was duly impressed."

"There's still a bit of Paddy left in me," owned Simon. "*I'm* impressed. Would you, as a change from sordid modern cases, be interested in my little historical puzzler? Come up to the Place for coffee, this evening, all the family. Try your professional wits on Squire Treverra's epitaphs. There's no special reason why they should, but they always sound like cryptograms to me. Anyhow, the whole library is interesting. Not many such families were literate enough to amass a collection like theirs."

"Thanks," said George, "we should like to, very much, if Miss Rachel has no objection to being invaded."

"Miss Rachel loves it. Surround her with personable young men, and she's in her element." He smiled at Dominic, presenting him gratis with this bouquet. "I'm sorry I made such shameless use of you just now. Thanks for taking it so neatly. It helped him to accept it, and frankly, I don't think it's going to be much of a show for kids, and I'd rather keep him out of it."

"As a matter of fact," confessed Dominic ruefully, "I *had* wanted to ask, only I didn't quite like to. But of course it's settled now, anyhow. I don't mind, if it makes Paddy feel he's had a fair hearing."

"I'm sorry to have had to do it, all the same. I suppose it wouldn't do to ask you to come along, after all? No, I'm afraid Paddy wouldn't forgive a dirty trick like that, and he'll be somewhere not far away."

"Couldn't possibly risk it," said Dominic firmly.

"But it really is a pity, because we *could* make room for *one* more sound man in the team." And lightly Simon turned his deep-brown eyes, in their shapely pits of fine wrinkles etched paler in the bronzed skin, and looked innocently at George. "So how about you, George? I'd be very glad to have you there. Will you come?"

Visitors to Treverra Place were treated to a personally conducted tour of the whole house and grounds, both of which, in their way, were well worth seeing. Miss Rachel, bright as a macaw in black silk and emeralds and a Chinese shawl, tapped her way valiantly ahead with the stick she used as an extension of her personality rather than an aid to navigation, and pointed out, even more meticulously than its beauties, the drawbacks and imperfections of her family seat. She loved visitors; they were allowed to miss nothing.

Treverra portraits filled the long galleries on the first floor, and stared from the lofty well of the staircase.

"Most of them very bad," said Miss Rachel, dismissing them with a wave of her wand. "All local work, we were not an artistic family, but we insisted on thinking we were." The listeners got the impression that in her own mind she had been there from the beginning. "There's just one very nice miniature here in the parlour—a young man."

"It would be," said Tamsin softly into Dominic's ear, bringing up the rear of the procession. But she said it with affectionate indulgence rather than cynically. In her own way she was very fond of her formidable old employer.

"The garden," announced Miss Rachel, pounding across the terrace and threatening it with the silver hilt of her stick, "is a disgrace. It is quite impossible to get proper gardeners these days. I am forced to make do with one idiot boy, and three days a week from the verger at St. Mary's. There's positively no relying on the younger generation. Trethuan promised he'd come in to-day and pick the apricots and Victoria plums. And has he put in an appearance? He has not. Never a sign of him, and never a word of excuse."

"Maybe he wanted to finish scything the churchyard extension to-day," suggested Simon vaguely, attendant at her heels. "He left it half-done yesterday, so the Vicar says."

"If he's going to be a jobbing gardener in addition to verger," insisted the old lady scornfully, "he should *be* one, and plan his time accordingly. He came in yesterday afternoon and picked just one tree of plums, and promised he'd be in to-day to finish the job. I was talking to him in the kitchen-garden not two minutes after you left here to go home to tea, Simon, and he said he'd only had an hour to spare, and he'd just looked in to let me know he'd give me the *whole* of to-day. And not a sign of him. You simply cannot rely on the young people nowadays."

"Trethuan is not much above fifty," explained Tamsin in Dominic's ear.

"And I particularly wanted to send some apricots down to Phil, while they're at their best. She has such a good hand with bottling."

"I tell you what," said Simon promptly, "get Paddy to come and pick them for Phil to-morrow, and keep him out of our hair. He's dying to get in on the act, it'll be a good idea to find him something to keep him out of mischief."

Miss Rachel halted at the low balustrade of the front terrace, spreading her Chinese silks in an expansive wave over the mock marble. Her shrewd old face had become suddenly as milkily still as a pond.

"Paddy?" she said, in a sweet, absent voice. "Absurd! Such a sensitive boy, I'm sure he wouldn't join you in your grave-hunt for any consideration. Certainly I'll get Phil to send him up for some apricots, but whatever makes you think he has any interest in your undertaking at St. Nectan's?"

Simon laughed aloud. "Just the fact that he came and asked if he could be there. Asked very nicely, too, but it didn't get him anywhere. It's no horror project, but still it isn't for growing boys."

She had resumed her march, but slowly and thoughtfully. Without looking at him she asked innocently: "When did he ask you?"

"This morning, around noon. Why?"

"Oh, nothing! I just found it hard to believe he'd do such a thing, that's all." After I had expressly forbidden it, she thought, in a majestic rage, but she kept her own counsel and her old face bland and benign. Something drastic will have to be done about Master Paddy. This cannot be allowed to go on. The child is *shockingly* spoiled. If Phil and Tim can't take him in hand, *I* shall have to.

"And this," declared Miss Rachel triumphantly, while the grandmotherly corner of her mind planned a salutary shock for Paddy Rossall, "this is our library."

She always brought her visitors to it by this way, through the great door from the terrace, springing on them magnificently the surprise of its great length and loftiness of pale oak panelling and pale oak bookshelves, the array of narrow full-length mirrors between the cases on the inner walls, and the fronting array of windows that poured light upon them. By any standards it was a splendid room, beautifully proportioned and beautifully unfurnished. There was Tamsin's desk at the far window of the range, and the big central table with its surrounding chairs, and two large and mutually contradictory globes, one at either end of the room. And all the rest was books.

On the nearer end of the long table a large, steaming coffee-tray had been deposited exactly ten seconds before they entered by the outer door; and the inner door was just closing smoothly after Miss Rachel's one elderly resident maid. When there were visitors to be impressed, the time-table in Treverra Place worked to the split second.

: :   : :

"There he is," said Simon, "the man himself."

The painting was small and dark and clumsy, a full-face presentation in the country style; commissioned portraits among small county families of the eighteenth century were meant to be immediately recognisable, and paid for accordingly. There was a short, livid scar across the angle of a square rat-trap of a jaw, redeemed by the liveliest, most humorous and audacious mouth Dominic had ever seen. A plain, ordinary face at first sight, until you looked at every feature in this same individual way, and saw how singular it was. The jaw could have been a pirate's, the large, uneven brow might have belonged to a justice of the peace, and in fact had, for several years, until the squire had felt it more tactful to withdraw from the bench. The eyes were the roving, adventurous eyes of a lawless poet, and that joyous mouth would have looked well on the young, the gallant, the irresistible Falstaff.

Simon stood back from the wall, and looked the most celebrated of the Treverras full in the eyes.

George thought : They really seem to be looking at each other, measuring each other, even communicating. And although they look so different, isn't there something intensely alike about them? Both privateers, a little off the regular track, not quite manageable by ordinary rules, not quite containable by ordinary standards.

"He had one ship trading across the Atlantic, and three or four small craft fishing and coasting here. And smuggling, of course. They all did it. It wasn't any crime to them, it was business and sport——"

"Could it be," whispered Dominic in Tamsin's ear, "that Simon has his tenses wrong?"

She turned her head so rapidly that the fine red hair fanned out and tickled his nose. She gave him a lightning look, and again evaded his eyes.

"I hope they got everything away safely last night," he said even more softly. He couldn't resist the innocent swagger, and it was hardly disobeying orders at all. This time she didn't look at him, but he saw her lip quiver and her cheek dimple, and she said to him out of the corner of a motionless mouth, like an old lag at exercise :

"You certainly are a sharp young man, Dominic Felse, be careful you don't cut yourself."

"And here's his wife. Morwenna, her name was."

"She was lovely," said Bunty, surveying the unexpected charcoal drawing on grey, rough paper, heightened with white chalk and red. Fragile but striking, like the creature it encompassed. Fine, fiery dark eyes, a delicately poised head balancing a sheaf of piled black hair.

Miss Rachel beamed satisfaction from the background.

" I used to be thought very like her when I was younger."

"Actually," murmured Tamsin in Dominic's ear, " she's the living image of Jan, if you cover up that jaw of his."

"And these are the famous epitaphs?" George stepped close to the two framed photographs on the wall below Morwenna's portrait.

> "' O Mortal Man, whom Fate——' "

"You'll find it easier from these transcriptions. Those photographs were made last time the church was cleared of sand, fifteen years or so ago. Whoever took them did a nice job on the angle of the light, and the lettering isn't much eroded, but it's eccentric. Here's the text."

Simon read aloud, in the full, rapt voice of self-forgetfulness, as though the reflected image of Treverra stirred within him; and it was not often, Tamsin told herself, watching, that Simon forgot himself.

> "' O Mortal Man, whom Fate may send
> To brood upon Treverra's End,
> Think not to find, beneath this Stone,
> Mute Witness, bleached, ambiguous Bone.
> Faith the intrepid Soul can raise
> And pilot through the trackless Maze,
> Pierce unappalled the Granite Gloom,
> The Labyrinth beyond the Tomb,
> And bring him forth to Regions bright,
> Bathed in the Warmth of Love and Light,
> Where year-long Summer sheds her Ease
> On golden Sands and sapphire Seas.
> There follow, O my Soul, and find
> Thy Lord as ever true and kind,
> And savour, where all Travellers meet,
> The last Love as the first Love sweet.'

"That was for himself. And this one is hers. Some say Jan wrote it before he died, knowing they wouldn't be parted long. Some say she wrote it herself in his style. Sometimes I think it's more remarkable than the other.

> "' *Carve this upon Morwenna's Grave:*
> NONE BUT THE BRAVE DESERVES THE BRAVE.
> *Shed here no Tears. No Saint could die*
> *More Blessed and Comforted than I.*
> *For I confide I shall but rest*
> *A Moment in this stony Nest,*
> *Then, raised by Love, go forth to find*
> *A Country dearer to my Mind,*
> *And touching safe the sun-bright Shore,*
> *Embrace my risen Lord once more'*."

There was a brief and curiously magical silence, and no one wanted to break it. It was not that the poetry was so lofty, but rather that it was so elusive, as though every phrase in it had at least two meanings, and therefore at any line you could lose your way, but if at every line you took the correct turning you would find yourself at the centre of a maze, always an achievement, and sometimes a revelation.

"Any reactions?" asked Simon, poking a deliberately brutal finger through the web of hallucination. "Apart from the fact that here was a bloke who knew his folk-verse and his Dryden equally well?"

Tamsin prodded Dominic in the ribs unexpectedly. "Go ahead!" she hissed in his ear. "Say something profound!"

Startled, he blurted out exactly what was in his mind. "They make the after-life sound like a Christmas sunshine cruise to the Bahamas."

CHAPTER III

FRIDAY MORNING

"You," SAID MISS RACHEL, waiting for Paddy in the arched gateway of the kitchen-garden with silver-hilted stick at the slope, like a superannuated angel drafted to the gate of paradise in an emergency, "you are a thoroughly bad boy."

"Yes," said Paddy in glum resignation, "I thought I should be." He hoisted the outsize basket from his carrier and dangled it sulkily. "Well, you won. I'm here, and I'll pick apricots, even if I won't like it. What more do you want?"

"Come inside here, and put that basket down for a few minutes. I want to talk to you."

He complied, but with an audible groan. He'd ridden up from the farm on his reluctant errand with nothing worse in his mind than scorn for all women and their conspiratorial tactics, a feeling which gave him a certain sense of detachment and superiority. A baby could have seen through this move to keep him away even from the sand-dunes on this of all mornings. His mother again, of course, enlisting Miss Rachel's aid. What else could it mean? Only women did things like that. Men came right out and said : "If I see you within a quarter of a mile of St. Nectan's I'll skin you." But women put their scheming heads together and concocted a job for you to do somewhere else.

"I suppose you and Mummy worked out how long it would take me to fill this thing," he said, dropping the basket on the grass, "and took jolly good care to make it an all-morning job. All right, I'll fill it. And she'll have to get down to it and bottle the lot to-day, and serve her right."

51

"Your mother has nothing whatever to do with this. If you want to blame anyone for it," she said grimly, "you can blame yourself and me—no one else. You went straight out from here, yesterday, and hunted out Simon. After I'd expressly told you not to! Didn't you?"

"All right," he said, roused and scowling, "I did. How did you know about it? But I'd have told you, anyhow, if you'd asked me."

"Simon let it out, last night. Oh, quite innocently, don't worry, *he* didn't know you'd gone flatly against my orders and your parents' wishes. Paddy Rossall, how *could* you!"

"They asked for it," said Paddy, goaded. "If you want to know, I *wasn't* going to go after Simon, by the time I got here I'd got over it, and it seemed mean and silly. But it didn't seem mean and silly to *her,* did it, to get together with you just to balk me? That's different, isn't it? It doesn't count if you gang up on your son, but it's a crime if you do the same to your mother."

"Now, you stop this nonsense this minute," commanded the old lady, quivering with indignation. "Your parents have a perfect right to check you—and to expect at least obedience from you, if nothing else. They're responsible for you, of course they're entitled to take whatever steps they think necessary for your good. You don't realise how much you owe to them, or how badly you're behaving to them. You take all their love and care for granted. Well, let me tell you, young man, if you had any gratitude in you, you'd never be able to think of enough ways to repay them for all they've done for you."

He couldn't bear it. To have the most secret, penitent and loving promptings of his heart ripped out and brandished in front of him, made cheap and public and sanctimonious like the disgusting parables in some old-fashioned moral book for children—it was too much. He reacted violently against it, with flooding colour and reckless rage, crying out things he didn't mean and didn't believe, in an effort to restore at least a balance of decency.

"So only one side's got any rights! What about *my* rights? Did I ask them to have me? *They* could have

helped it, couldn't they? But *I* couldn't, I didn't have any
choice. I'm their *son*, remember?"

Whether Miss Rachel can be said at this point to have
taken any actual decision to resort to extreme measures, or
whether she was quite simply pushed over the edge of
action before she realised it, the result was the same. She
drew herself to her full modest height, looking more like
Queen Victoria than Paddy had ever seen her, and in a
half-smothered voice of shocked and royal rage, with judgment in every syllable, she said what could never again be
unsaid.

"*No*," said Miss Rachel, full into his angry, miserable
face, "you are *not*!"

   : :   : :

His first instinct was quite simply not to hear her, to pick
up his basket and back out of this argument now, before
events overwhelmed him. Such a thing could not have
been said, and therefore it had not been said. He cast one
desperate glance round him, looking for a way of escape.

"Which tree am I supposed to—to start——"

It was no use, the words were still there in his ears,
stinging like an echo, and he could not get rid of them by
pretending they were mere meaningless sound. His second
impulse was to laugh. If this was her way of punishing him,
it was a splendidly silly one. But she stood there squarely
before him, watching his face intently and maintaining her
unrelenting gravity, and there wasn't the ghost of a chance
that she was just being spiteful. The laugh collapsed in
ruins. He stared at her, his eyes enormous and stricken,
pushing the inconceivable thing away from him with one
last convulsive effort at regaining the normal ground of
everyday.

"It isn't true," he said passionately.

"However angry I may be with you," said Miss Rachel
harshly, "I wouldn't lie to you."

"No," he owned forlornly, "that's right, you wouldn't."
He began to shake. "But I *must* be, I *have* to be, I *am*. I
can't start being somebody else——"

"Now, don't be silly. You're old enough to understand

these things, and there's no need to get upset about it. Here, come and sit down, and listen to me."

She took him by the arm, unresisting, and led him to the stone seat under the sunny wall, and there plumped him down before her, diminished strangely in years, a lost small boy. Big, stunned eyes stared at, and round, and through her, and saw nothing at all. She tapped his cheek lightly, and nothing whatever happened. It took quite a sharp slap to startle those eyes back into focusing, and jolt a spark of warmth and feeling back into the fixed face.

" Oh, come along, now, you know people often adopt children, there's nothing so strange about it. Tim and Phil adopted you, you're *not* their own child. They took you legally, as a very young baby, from a friend of theirs whose wife had died. And don't run away with the idea that you were chosen for the part, either. They took you against their inclinations at the time, out of pity, because your father didn't want you."

That brought the live and angry colour back to his cheeks, and a flare to his eyes that still looked like mutiny, even in the face of the firing-squad.

" Yes, you heard me correctly. Didn't want you! He could perfectly well have afforded to pay for proper care for you, but a baby was a nuisance to him. He took advantage of the fact that Phil had lost a child of her own, and couldn't have another, and he worked on her feelings until she took you off his hands. That's how much your father cared about you. Tim and Phil took you out of pity, and they've loved and cared for you ever since. And this is how you behave to them in return! You'll see," said Miss Rachel with stern emphasis, " if you go on like this, *no one* will be able to love you."

Somewhere deep inside him that started an echo that hurt and frightened him. He shut himself fiercely about it to contain the fear and pain, unwilling to give her the satisfaction of having moved him.

" I don't believe it," he said obstinately. But he did,

that was the worst part of it, that he couldn't even hope
for it to be a lie. "You're making it up, just to scare me."

"You know quite well I'm doing nothing of the kind.
And there's no occasion at all for being scared. You're
theirs now, and you know they love you, even if you don't
always deserve it. And you know that everything will go
on just the same as always. This doesn't alter anything.
Except, I hope, the way *you*'ll look at things from now on."

Doesn't alter anything! Only the whole of his world, and
worse still, the heart in his body and the mind in his head,
and the memory of a lordly childhood he had always supposed to be simple, unassailable, and his by right.

In the flat, practical voice of shock, which she had no
way of recognising, he said: "Why did they never tell
me?, I wouldn't have minded so much if I'd known all
along, I could have got used to it."

"That was their mistake. I know it, I always told them
so. They thought you need never know, because it happened just about the time they were thinking of moving
here to Pentarno. By the time they realised how foolish
they'd been, they'd left it so late they didn't know how to
go about it. So they kept quiet and hoped for the best.
But *I* think it's high time you knew what you really owe
to them. Maybe now you'll show a little more gratitude
and consideration."

"I didn't know I wasn't. I mean—I didn't know I had
to be more grateful than other boys——"

"Now, there's no need to feel like that about it. You
just think it over quietly, while you pick the apricots for
your mother, and see if you can't make up your mind to
behave a bit better to her in future."

He looked at his hands, which were gripping the edge of
the stone seat so hard that the knuckles were white. He
wasn't sure whether he could detach them without having
them start shaking again, but he tried it with one, cautiously,
and it was quite steady. He picked up the basket. Everything seemed to work much the same as before, and yet he
felt a long, long way from his own body, as though he were
looking on at a play.

" All right. Which tree shall I start on?"

She told him, piloted him to it, not without certain careful sidelong glances at the chilled quietness of his face, and left him to his labours, firmly determined not to fuss over him now and undo the good she had done. He'd needed a sharp lesson. All boys get above themselves at times, even the nicest. It would be disastrous to hang over him anxiously at this stage, and betray the fact that he had only to manufacture a look of distress to twist her round his finger again. So she tapped away stubbornly out of the kitchen-garden, without once looking back. It was going to take her the whole of the next hour to convince herself that she had done the right, the necessary, the only possible thing, and there was not now, and never would be in the future, any cause to regret it. But she would manage it eventually, and then forget that she had ever been in doubt. What she did must be right, as it always had been.

Paddy set the basket on the edge of the gravel path, and began methodically to strip the apricot tree. Somewhere infinitely distant and dark, his mind groped feverishly after the full awful implications of what he had heard. Fifteen is a vulnerable age. Once the possibility was presented to him, he found it only too easy to believe that nobody could love him, and to imagine that nobody ever had. When he came to consider himself in this new light, stripped of privilege, he didn't find himself a particularly lovable specimen. The people you rely on, the people you're sure of, even though you don't deserve them—what happens when you suddenly lose them? Like having the world jerked out from under your feet as neatly as a mat.

Now he wasn't sure of them or of anything. Oh, he knew, just as positively as ever, that they were wonderful, that he adored them, that they would never let him down. They'd always been marvellous to him, and always would be; that wasn't what dismayed him. But now he found himself horribly afraid that it was only out of pity for his forlorn estate, unwanted by his father, a rejected nuisance, badly in need of someone to take pity on him. The shock of feeling himself uprooted, of not even knowing who or what he was, was bad enough. But the shock of turning to look again at the parents he had hitherto taken for granted as his undisputed, cherished and misused property, of seeing them suddenly strange, forbearing and kind, and not his at all, only suffering him out of the goodness of their hearts, of feeling his inside liquefy with fearful doubts as to whether they could ever truly have loved him or felt him to be theirs—this was too much for him to grasp or face. He shrank from it into protective numbness, clinging desolately to the job he had been given to do, and dreading the time when the shell of habit would crack and fall away, and leave him naked to the chill of what he knew. Furiously he plucked apricots he was not aware of seeing and loaded them into the basket he hardly knew he was filling.

:: ::

" You might," said Miss Rachel, making an unexpected appearance in the library at about half past eleven, " take out some ginger-beer and cake for Paddy. I daresay he'd like something by now."

" I daresay he would," agreed Tamsin, " if he hasn't eaten himself sick on apricots. I know which I'd rather have."

" Paddy isn't afraid of spoiling his figure," said Miss Rachel nastily.

Tamsin rose from her work with a sigh, and took the peace-offering the old lady had prepared with her own hands. And very nice, too, she thought. Chocolate layer cake, and the almond biscuits he likes best. What did he do to be in such high favour to-day? Or what's she trying to smooth over? Come to think of it, why doesn't she take it out to him herself?

She was back very quickly, and still carrying the tray. " He's not there."

" Nonsense, he must be there." Miss Rachel's resolutely confident face grew indignant at the suggestion that things could slip out of the comfortable course she had laid down for them. "You haven't looked properly."

"Under every leaf. He isn't there, and his bike isn't there, and his basket isn't there. And the apricots from that first tree aren't there, either. He must have worked like a demon. Probably to get away and down to the dunes before the matinée's over."

"Ah!" said Miss Rachel, seizing gratefully on a solution which permitted her to keep her self-righteousness, her indignation against him, and her cheering conviction that children were as tough as badgers. "That's probably what it is. The little wretch! I just hope Tim will send him home with a flea in his ear."

:   :   :   :

They rode down to the church promptly at ten, in Tim's Land-Rover and Simon's grey Porsche, dropping from the coastal road through the dunes by a pebble-laid track among the tamarisk hedges, silted over here and there by fine drifts of sand. The tang of salt and the straw-tinted pallor of salt-bleached grasses surrounded them, the fine lace of the tamarisks patterned the cloudless but windy aquamarine sky on either side. The small car led, with Simon driving it and George beside him. The Land-Rover, used to being taken anywhere and everywhere by Tim, ambled after like a good-natured St. Bernard making believe to chase a greyhound pup. Tim and Sam Shubrough up in front, the Vicar behind for ballast, with the additional tackle they had brought along in case of need.

A formidable team, thought George, considering them. Simon and George himself would have passed for presentable enough physical specimens by most standards, but here they were the light-weights. Tim stood an inch or two less than either of them, but was half as broad again, and in hard training from the outdoor life he had led in all weathers. Sam Shubrough was a piece of one of the harder red sandstones of the district, animated. But the greatest surprise was the Reverend Daniel Polwhele.

The Vicar of St. Mary's, Maymouth, stood six feet three

in his socks, and looked like the product of several genera-
tions of selective breeding from the families of Cornish
wrestlers. He wore the clothes of his calling with a splendid simplicity, and was neither set apart by them nor in
any way apologetic for them. Shouldering a couple of
crowbars, he looked as much at home as with a prayer-
book, because he approached everything in the world with
a large, curious and intelligent innocence, willing to investigate and be investigated.

He was probably forty-five, but dating him was the last
thing you'd think of trying to do. He had a broad, bony
Cornish face, without guile but inscrutable, and a lot of
untidy, grizzled dark hair that he forgot to have cut,
and eyes as thoughtful, direct and disconcerting as a small
boy's, but more tolerant.

The great waste of sand opened before them, and the
great waste of sea beyond, a vast still plane and a vast
vibrating plane. Through the tamarisk fronds they saw
to the left the fanged head of the Dragon jutting out to sea,
and nearer, at the southern end of the length of Pentarno
sands, the low pebbly ridge of the Mortuary, dark with
the rim of weed that built up there with every incoming
tide. To their right was the clean, bright sand where
young Paddy ran down to bathe every morning and every
afternoon during the holidays. And here, tucked away
on their left at the blown limit of the dunes, was St. Nectan's
church. They saw it first by the small, squat tower and
the little peaked roof over the empty lantern where once
there had been a bell. Then, as they entered the small,
cleared bowl, the whole building stood before them; very
small, plain as a barn, with tiny, high lancet windows
pierced here and there without plan or pattern, a narrow,
crooked, porchless door with a scratched dog-tooth border
almost eroded away, and a rounded tympanum with a crude
little carving that could barely be distinguished now.

" Saxon, all the base of the walls," said the Vicar,
bounding out of the back of the Land-Rover and approaching George as he stood contemplating the relic. " Windows
and door and lantern very early Norman. The roof was

re-slated not long before they gave it up as a bad job and built St. Mary's. The foundations go right down to the rock. We keep losing this, but St. Mary's will fall down first."

The permanence and elemental quality of the sea pervaded the little church, the laboriously cleared graveyard with its stunted stones and erased names, the feathery curtains of tamarisks. Only the large grey hulk of the Treverra tomb, a stone cube rising about three feet above the surrounding ground, still obstinately asserted its own identity.

Before the tomb there was a railed-in pit, stone-lined and narrow, like a Victorian area. The iron gate swung freely on its newly-oiled hinges, and the fresh drift of sand was already filming over the steps of the staircase that descended to the low, broad door.

"I thought we should be sure to have an audience," said Simon, coming from the Porsche with a large iron key in his hand.

Tim laughed. "We have. Don't you know 'em yet? Half Pentarno and a fair sprinkling of Maymouth is deployed wherever there's cover along the coast road, moving in on us quietly right now. By the time we're down the steps and inside they'll be massing all round the rim. Only just within sight, they won't cramp you, but they won't miss a thing."

"One of my choirboys," said the Vicar brightly, "borrowed my binoculars this morning. I didn't ask him why. I fancy most of the trebles are up on the Dragon's Head, passing them round. It's more fun that way. Shall we go down?"

They already had their gear piled outside the sunken door. Simon trod gently down the steps, disturbing the furls of blown sand, and fitted Miss Rachel's key into the huge lock. It turned with ready smoothness, a fact on which, George noted, nobody commented. Sam Shubrough's benign red face was serene in ambush behind his noble whiskers, his eyes as placid as the sea. They entered the vault, letting in daylight with them to a segment of rock flooring, thinly and idly patterned with coils of sand that must have drifted under the door. It fitted closely, or there would surely have been much more. A well-sealed place, dry and clean, the walls faced with stone slabs, shutting out even the saltness of the sea air. Treverra had made himself snug.

Tim switched on the electric lamp he was carrying, and set it on the stone ledge that ran all round the walls at shoulder-height. Sam added a second one at the other side. And there they were, the two massive stone coffins, each set upon a plinth carved clear and left standing when the vault was cut deep into the rock. They occupied the whole centre of the chamber between them, a narrow passage separating them, a narrow space clear all round them. There was nothing else in the vault.

Plain altar tombs, their corners moulded into a cluster of pillars, the lips of their lids decorated with a scroll-work of leaves and vines, and a tablet on each lid brought to a high finish to carry the engraved epitaph. By these they were identifiable, even if the one coffin had not been larger than the other, and perhaps two or three inches higher.

" O Mortal Man——"

This was Treverra. And the other one, close to his side as in life, was the lady, that frail beauty with the brilliant and daring face. She must have been every inch his match, thought George tracing the deliberate misquotation from Dryden spelled out in challenging capitals over her breast :

" NONE BUT THE BRAVE DESERVES THE BRAVE."

Did a man ever think of that? Surely not! It was a woman making that claim for herself. Not wanting to be understood; wanting, in fact, not to be understood, but delighting in the risk. Why should she give that impression even in dying? She pined away. Only somehow it hadn't looked like a pining face.

The Vicar hefted the crowbars into the tomb. He stood holding them upright by his side, like the faithful sentinel, and looked again, long and thoughtfully, at the two coffins.

"I'd like to say a prayer first."

He prayed with his head unstooped and his eyes open, and in his own unorthodox way.

"Help us if we're doing well," he said, "and forgive us if we're not. Lord, let there be peace on all here, living and dead." He looked at the bold words on Morwenna's coffin, with respect and liking in his face. "And reunion for all true lovers," he said.

Simon said: "Amen!"

"And now, how do you want to handle it?"

Simon disposed his team as practically as the Vicar prayed, and with the same sense of purpose.

"I thought we could easily lever the lid from Jan's coffin over to rest on hers. It's more than broad enough to span the space between without overbalancing, and the drop's not more than two and a half inches. We'll cover her over with these thick felts—I brought them down on purpose—we don't want to damage either stone. Let's have two of you over on Morwenna's side. Right. We three will hoist the stone up on the clear side first, and you can get some thin wedges in. Then we'll see if there's a deep rim to deal with, and ease your side out gradually if there is."

George was at the head of the tomb, the Vicar in the middle, Simon at the foot. They got their crows started into the well-fitted chink of the stone, and eased it enough to get the first wedges in. After that it was merely a matter of patience. There was a rim to lift free on all sides, but a shallow one, and they got it clear without difficulty.

"It isn't so massive," said Tim, surprised. "Two of us could hoist it off in no time if we didn't have to be so careful about damaging it."

"True enough, but we do." Simon felt along the under edge where his crow had prised, and grimaced. "Matter of fact, it has chipped a bit. Hmm, here, too. Not much, but it seems to fret easily."

The Vicar measured the thickness of the stone slab with

an unimpressed eye, and found it thinner than he had supposed. He stooped and set his shoulder under its deep overhang, and hoisted experimentally, and the thing perceptibly shifted.

"We could lift it, Simon. Between the five of us, and taking it steadily together, now she's out of the socket we could manhandle her over. Try it!"

Simon eyed the stone doubtfully, and added another thickness of felt to the protective covering over Morwenna. "All right, we can but try. One at each corner, and I'll take the middle here. Everybody set? Here we come, then. Gently—heave!"

The stone moved, slid along in response to their hoist a couple of inches, and disclosed a hair-line of darkness along the near edge of the coffin as the overhanging lip drew clear.

"It's coming! Right, together—heave!" The hair-line of blackness became a pencil, an ebony ruler. Out of it came a breath of cold and the odour of the sea and of dust. Strange, the two together, as though the inimical elements had settled down together in the grave. "Again, heave!"

"Child's play!" said Sam cheerfully, and shifted his large feet to brace himself for the next hoist.

"Once more—heave!" The stone slid with their persuasion, and again settled, and this time as they relaxed their efforts it swung in delicate counter-balance, ready at a touch to tilt gently and ponderously, and come to rest against the felt padding on the lady's tomb. Nine inches of uncovered dark gaped below George's face, and the odour, faint but persistent, made his nostrils dilate and quiver. A more precisely defined odour now, not just the vague salt tang of the sea. Something more homely, and extraordinarily elusive—he thought, in a sequence of kaleidoscopic images, of sheep in salt pastures, of wire-haired terriers in the rain, of washing Dominic's woollies sometimes, long years ago, when Bunty had been ill. *Damp cloth! Woollen cloth!*

"Once more, and let her down gently. Ready—heave!"

Over slid the stone, and nested snugly on top of Morwenna's coffin, only its edge still propped upon the side of Treverra's own uncovered grave. The light of the two lamps fell obliquely into the stony space, and they all loosed their hold of the stone and leaned forward eagerly, craning to see what they had unveiled.

Only George, though with equal alacrity and a gasp as sharp as any, lunged back instead of forward. For that last strenuous lift and thrust had brought him up lying across the open coffin, almost face to face with the man who occupied it, as the stone slid from between them. The long, gaunt bony pallor of a lantern face gaped at him open-eyed from the dark, heavy jaw sagging towards a broad, barrel-staved chest in a dark grey pullover. Large, raw-boned hands jutted from the slightly short sleeves of an old black jacket, and lay half-curled against long black-clad thighs. And the smell of damp cloth and damp wool and damp human hair gushed up into their faces and sent them all into recoil after George.

Amazed and aghast, they stared and swallowed.

"If that's Treverra," said George with conviction, "I'm a Dutchman!"

The Vicar said: "Lord, have mercy on us all when the day comes! It isn't Treverra, but it is Trethuan."

"You know him?" George looked round at them all and saw by their appalled faces that he was, indeed, the only person present who did not know the incumbent of the coffin.

"I should. He's—he was—my verger at St. Mary's."

George stared down at the long, lank body that lay so strangely shallowly in the stone pit, and his mind went back some hours, after an evasive memory, and recaptured it, and was confounded. It seemed Miss Rachel had complained unjustly of the unreliability of the young. Her truant gardener, even if he had not been able to communicate it, had had the best of all reasons for not turning up yesterday. He had picked his last apricot, and scythed his last churchyard. He lay, minus one shoe and sock, and reeking of the clammy, harsh damp of sea-water from feet to hair, stone dead in Jan Treverra's coffin.

::   ::

"Lift him out," said Sam urgently, starting out of his daze. "He may not be dead."

"He's dead. Whoever he is, however he got here, he's dead enough. Don't touch him." George looked at Simon, looked at the Vicar across the coffin. Four intent, strained faces stared back at him with stunned eyes. "I'm sorry, but it looks as if this has got out of hand. Out of our hands, anyhow. We've got a body here that was apparently alive a couple of days ago, and is very dead now. I've got no official standing here. Do you mind if I take charge for the moment? I suspect—I'm pretty sure—it isn't going to be for long."

"Whatever you say," agreed Simon in a shaken voice. "This wasn't in my brief."

"Then leave him where he is. Don't move anything. Tim, bring that lamp over, and let's have a careful look in here."

Shocked into silence, Tim brought it, and tipped its light full in upon the dead man. George felt carefully at the well-worn, respectable black suit, the lank, dun-coloured hair, the hand-knitted pullover, the laces and sole of the one remaining shoe. All of them left on his fingers the clinging, sticky feel of salt. He felt down past the bony shoulder, and touched a flat surface beneath the body, not cold and final like the stone, but with the live, grained feel of wood about it.

"I thought he was lying very high. There's a wooden coffin below him." He tapped on it, and the small resulting sound was light and hollow. "Not very substantial, just a shell to go inside the stone. That should be Treverra. But this one——"

"There appears to be some injury to his head," said the Vicar, low-voiced. "Do you think——?"

"I *think* he drowned in the sea, but the doctors will settle that. Shine the light here, Tim."

Tim illuminated the bony, dark-skinned face. A darker, mottled stain covered the outer part of the socket of the left eye, the lower temple and the cheek-bone, the mark of a large, broken bruise.

"Could he have got that in the sea?" Sam's big voice was muted.

"I don't think so. I think it was done before death. And I think," he said, looking round them all and stepping back from the coffin, "we're going to have to turn this over at once to the Maymouth police. They'd better have a look at the whole set-up. Because it looks very much as if they've got a murder on their hands."

There was a moment of absolute silence and stillness; then Simon heaved a cautious breath and dusted the powdering of stone from his hands.

"One of us had better take the car and go and telephone," he said in the most practical of voices. "Will you go, George, or shall I?"

: :   : :

But the most incomprehensible thing of all about the St. Nectan project came later still, past noon, when the photographers and the experts and the police surgeon had all had their way with the Treverra tomb, and the long, lank body of Zebedee Trethuan, verger and jobbing gardener, had been taken out on a covered stretcher and driven away in an ambulance, watched silently and avidly by a gallery of fishermen, children, respectable housewives and solid townspeople from all the dunes around, and no doubt just as eagerly by all the trebles of St. Mary's choir, fighting over the Vicar's binoculars on top of the Dragon's Head.

They were left with the plain, light wooden coffin on which he had lain; and at the first touch the lid of it gave to their hands, and came away, uncovering—surely, this time?—the last resting-place of Jan Treverra. And there they were, the expected bones.

This body had certainly been there longer than its bed-fellow. It was almost a skeleton, shreds of perished clothing drifted about the long bones and the dried and mummified flesh that remained to it. But had it, on closer inspection, really been there for two centuries and more? It had a hasty and tumbled appearance, with no composed, hieratic dignity. The fragments of cloth still had enough nature left in them to show a texture and a colour; a colour which had been very dark navy blue, a texture that looked suspiciously like thick, solid modern woollen, meant to withstand all weathers. And here, about the chest, clung bits of disintegrating knitted stuff.

Among Treverra's eccentricities it had never been recorded that he wished to be buried in a fisherman's Meltons and a seaman's jersey.

By the middle of that Friday afternoon it was all over Maymouth that Jan Treverra's tomb had yielded not one body, but two; and that, positively though quite incomprehensibly, neither of them was Jan Treverra.

CHAPTER IV

FRIDAY AFTERNOON

DETECTIVE-SERGEANT HEWITT was pure Maymouth from his boots to his sober utilitarian hair-cut, a stocky, square man of middle age with a vaguely sad countenance, who used few words, but in some curious fashion turned other people voluble. In taking his last look round the Treverra vault before they locked it and left it to its ravished quietness, he said nothing at all. Only his solemn eyes lingered thoughtfully along the propped edge of the stone lid, with its specks of pallor where the iron had bitten into the stone; and Tim, following their reproachful survey, said apologetically: "I know, it's a pity we had to use crowbars and foul up the possible traces. But we couldn't possibly have *known*——" The grieved gaze moved lower, to the trampled patterns in the dust of the floor, and five pairs of feet did their best to appear smaller. "I'm afraid we have rather driven the herds over everything," said Simon ruefully. "It was dead smooth when we came in, though —just a blown layer of sand, as usual."

"Yes, well—if you gentlemen will go along with Snaith to the police station, right away, we'd like to have statements from all of you. Your individual observations may help us." He didn't sound hopeful, but he probably never did. "Mr. Felse, if you wouldn't mind, I'd like to have you along with me for a call on the way. We'll join the others in half an hour or so."

"Glad to, if I can be any help," said George.

"And I'll take the key, Mr. Towne." Simon surrendered it, and watched it turned in the great lock, with a soundless efficiency which did not fail to register with the Detective-Sergeant. "I see you've been preparing for to-day. This is the key from the Place?"

"Yes, the only one, as far as I know. I've had it three days now. Miss Rachel gave it to me when I wanted to bring down some of the gear."

"Yes, I gathered from what you said just now that you'd been in the vault before to-day. How often?"

"Twice. On Wednesday morning—the Vicar was with me that time—we came down to clear the steps and clean and oil the lock, and tried the key to be sure how it worked. But we didn't go farther then than just inside the doorway." And that, thought George, was probably when Simon spotted the illicit stores there, hence his discreet withdrawal, and the public declaration of his programme that evening. Nor had he actually said that they had in fact cleaned and oiled the lock, merely that they had come here with that intention. This job at least had proved unnecessary. "Then I came in again yesterday afternoon, and dumped those sheets of felt." To make sure that the hint had been taken?

"Notice anything at all different then? Or when you came in to-day?"

Simon considered. "Not that I recollect."

"You didn't sweep the floor clean of sand?"

"No. Never occurred to me, even if I'd had a broom.

I was surprised how dry and clean it was in here, only a blown layer of sand. Just like now—except for our hoof-marks, of course," said Simon ruefully.

"Ah, well, you'll have time to think it over. Mr. Felse and I will be with you shortly."

They climbed the narrow steps on which the sand whisked softly like blown spray, and closed the latchless gate upon the solitude so bewilderingly void of Treverra, and so over-populated with others who had no business there. The Land-Rover and the Porsche set off for the police station in Maymouth, Detective-Constable Snaith, son of a long line of fishermen, ensconced in George's place beside Simon. Only when the little convoy was well away did Hewitt climb ponderously into his Morris.

"We shan't be going far out of our way. Just along the quay to where his girl lives. I thought a detached witness might come in handy, if you don't mind being used. I've known Rose since she was first at school. Being this close to a place has its drawbacks, as well as its advantages."

"I know," said George, thinking of his own home village of Comerford, where every face was known to him. "Trethuan's daughter?"

"Yes, only relative, as far as I know. She's been married a year to a decent young fellow, Jim Pollard. Fisherman, of course, they all are. Lives about three minutes' walk from where Trethuan lived."

"Alone, I take it? Now that the girl's married?"

"Yes, alone. Did for himself most of the time, and Rose did the real cleaning for him. Thought I'd better see her and tell her myself."

It should have been a daunting prospect, but though he maintained his aspect of professional and permanent dis-couragement, Hewitt did not, in fact, appear at all daunted. And wasn't there, perhaps, something in that gaunt, power-ful, unprepossessing corpse in Treverra's tomb that ruled out any harrowing possibilities of family lamentation? There are people it's almost impossible to love, however the blood may struggle to do its duty.

They drove over the neck of the Dragon, the coastal road

rising to its highest point near to the hotel. A fair portion
of the juvenile population of Maymouth was still deployed
along the cliff paths looking towards Pentarno; no doubt
armed with fruit and sandwiches, and with an organised
errand-service for ice-cream. Then the road dipped again,
and the slate-grey cottages of the upper town closed in
upon it, backgrounds for their small, crowded flower-
gardens, that blazed with every possible colour. From the
steep High Street they could see the harbour below them,
locked between the huge bulk of the Dragon's Head and
the crook of the mole, all the invisible streets doddering
down towards it, seen only as thread-like channels between
the slate roofs. Uniformly grey from this aerial view, the
houses flowered into apple-blossom pinks and forget-me-not
blues as the car descended, every shade of peach and prim-
rose and pale green, foaming with window-boxes full of
geraniums.

In the square, four-sided about an ugly Victorian fountain
and embattled with solid shop-fronts, they saw the Porsche
and the Land-Rover parked. But Hewitt drove on im-
perturbably, down towards the harbour, and the clusters of
colour-washed houses that clung like barnacles to the rocks
along the sea-front.

A row of leaning cottages, six in all, propped their backs
against the outlying rocks of the Dragon, and stared out
to sea over beached boats and a flurry of gulls. Each was
painted its own individual shade, two different pinks, a
daffodil yellow, one blue, one green, and one dazzlingly
white. Hewitt parked the car on the cobbled shoulder
of the quay, and led the way to the second pink house. A
little horse-shoe knocker rapped on the jet-black door.
The whole row looked like toys in a child's box.

Rose Pollard opened the door. At first glance Rose looked
like a round, soft, primrose-haired doll to go with the toy
house, but this illusion lasted only for the fraction of a
second it took her large, inquiring eyes to recognise Hewitt.
The round face, as delicately-coloured as a nursery-rhyme
dairy-maid's, nevertheless had some form and character
when it sharpened into awareness; and there was nothing

doll-like about the small, bright flares of fear that sprang up in her eyes. Hewitt was known to everyone, as surely as he knew everyone. But why should she be frightened at the very sight of him? Or, wondered George ruefully, was it occupational naivety on his part even to ask such a question?

She mastered her face, and rather nervously invited them in. The front door gave directly into the tiny living-room, which was as neat and frilly as the exterior of the house suggested it would be. The mind behind that pretty, plaintive face was probably itself furnished in the same innocent fashion; not much style, and no sophistication, but shining with cleanness and prettied up with pouffes, scatter cushions and net curtains. Not a very clever girl, but meant to be gay and bright; and certainly not meant to habit with things or people or thoughts that could frighten her.

"Sorry to butt in on you at dinner, Jim," said Hewitt placidly, looking over her shoulder at the young man who rose from the table as they entered. "Just a few things I ought to ask you and Rose, if you've got a minute or two to give me."

"That's all right," said Jim Pollard, uncoiling his tall young person awkwardly. "We're finished, Mr. Hewitt. I was late coming in, or we'd have been all cleared away. Is there something the matter?"

He was a brown, freckled boy in a loose sweater and faded dungarees, with a face that must normally have been pleasant, good-natured and candid, but at this moment was clouded with the slight blankness and uncertainty consequent upon being visited by the police. It happens to the most law-abiding, it need mean nothing; but the barrier is instantly there, and the trouble is that there's never any telling what's behind it.

"Well, there's just this matter of Mr. Trethuan's movements," said Hewitt with nicely calculated vagueness. "Have you seen him to-day?"

Rose said: "No!" She moved nearer to her husband, and the small, wary lights in her eyes burned paler and taller. The boy said: "No," too, but in a mystified, patient tone, ready to wait for enlightenment. His steady frown never changed.

"Or yesterday? Well, when did you last see him, Mrs. Pollard?"

"Wednesday morning," she said, "when I went in to clean. I usually go in Wednesdays and Saturdays and give the house a going-over. He was finishing his breakfast when I went. I only saw him for a few minutes, then he went off to work."

"And you haven't seen him since? You don't know whether he came home that night?"

"Why should she?" said Jim Pollard evenly. "He's capable, he can look after himself. Often we don't see him for days on end."

"Even though he only lives just round the corner in Fore Street?"

"Maybe he does, but it is round the corner, we don't run into one another going in and out of the back doors. Thank God!" said Jim with deliberation, eyeing Hewitt darkly from under his corrugated brow.

"Now, Jim!" said Rose in a faint murmur of protest.

"Never mind: Now, Jim! Mr. Hewitt knows as well as you do there's no love lost between your old man and me. Less I see of him, the better. I might as well say so."

"So you might, lad," agreed Hewitt placatingly. "Then I take it you don't know anything about him since your missus saw him Wednesday morning?"

"No, I don't, Mr. Hewitt. I haven't set eyes on him since last Sunday in church. What's he done to interest you?"

Rose shrank under her husband's hand, and turned her head to shoot him a look of panic entreaty, but all his attention was on Hewitt, and whatever his own disquiet, he seemed to feel nothing of the urgency of hers.

"It isn't what he's *done*," said Hewitt heavily. "I'm afraid this is going to be a bit of a shock to you, Rose, my girl. Your father was found this morning by Mr. Towne and the others, when they went to open the Treverra vault——"

Her soft, round face lost its colour in one gasp, blanched to a dull, livid pallor. Her eyes stared, enormous and sick. Her lips moved soundlessly, saying: "In the vault——?" Then her mouth shook, and she crammed half her right fist into it, like a child, and swallowed a muted cry.

"Yes, in the vault. He's dead, Rose. I'm sorry!"

Her knees gave way under her, and Jim caught her in his arms and held her, turning her to him gently. "Now, love, don't! Come on, now, Rose, hold up!"

She clung to him and wept, but they were not tears of any particularly poignant grief, only of excitement, and nervous tension, and—was it possible?—relief. She cried easily, freely, with no convulsive physical struggle. Even fear was submerged, or so it seemed, until Hewitt added rather woodenly: "It looks like foul play. We shall have a lot of work to do on the case before we have full information. We'll be in close touch with you. And if you can think of anything that may help to fill in his movements in the last days, we shall be glad to have it."

"Are you trying to tell us," demanded Jim Pollard, scowling over his wife's blonde head, "that old Zeb's been *murdered*?"

"Yes," said Hewitt mildly, "that's exactly what I'm trying to tell you."

Then they were both absolutely still; and perceptibly, even while they stood motionless, they withdrew into themselves, and very carefully and gently closed the doors to shut the world and Hewitt out. Jim tightened his hold on his wife, and that was the only reaction there was to be seen in him. Rose—and how much more significant that was!—Rose drew a long, slow, infinitely cautious breath, and stopped crying on the instant. She needed her powers now for more urgent purposes.

: :   : :

"Well," said Hewitt, turning the car uphill again at the corner of Fore Street, "what do you make of them?"

"Rose is frightened," said George. "Very frightened.

Her husband, as far as I can see, is merely normally cagey. When the police come around asking about one of the family, nobody's at his most expansive. But what's more interesting is that she was frightened before you even asked a question. And most frightened of all when you mentioned the Treverra vault, before—I think—she realised you meant he was dead."

"Ah!" said Hewitt cryptically, but with every appearance of satisfaction with his own thoughts. "You do notice things, don't you? I just wanted to know. Then you can't very well have missed the broom-marks."

"Broom-marks?" said George carefully.

"On the steps of the vault. And the floor, too. Mr. Towne didn't have a broom down there, but somebody did. Very delicately done, but still it showed. Take another look at the corners, where none of you stepped to-day. Somebody had moved around that room, and then carefully swept it, and dusted a layer of sand over it again to wipe out the prints. Almost impossible to do it as smoothly as time and the wind do it."

He slanted a knowing look along his shoulder at George's wooden face.

"Ah, come off it! I'm not in the excise. It's a murderer I'm after. I'm not interested in what a whole bunch of people were doing in there just ahead of the researchers. Murder is a solitary crime, Mr. Felse. No easy-going muddle of local brandy-runners put Trethuan in Jan Treverra's coffin, that I'll bet my life on. But what I am interested in——"

"Yes?" said George with respect.

"Is the key they let themselves in with. And who else may have had access to it."

: :   : :

"Oh, no," said the Vicar, emerging from deep thought, "I don't think he had any actual *enemies*. Only people who're positive enough to have friends have enemies. When you're as glum and morose as he was, people just give up and go away." He glanced round the circle of attentive faces in Hewitt's office, and ruffled his untidy hair. "I don't think he wanted or needed liking, you know. Not everyone does."

Hewitt gave him a brief, baffled look, and returned with a sigh to his summing-up.

"Well, we've got him to Wednesday morning. He worked on the churchyard extension, hedge-clipping and then scything, all the morning, or at least he was at work on it when Mr. Polwhele and Mr. Towne came home to lunch after their trip down to the vault. He had his meal in the vicarage kitchen, and went back to work, and he was there when Mr. Towne left to go on to Treverra Place. Both Mr. Towne and Mr. Polwhele agree that would be about a quarter to three. Mr. Towne exchanged words with Trethuan in the churchyard as he walked through. Mr. Polwhele saw him put away his tools shortly afterwards and leave. That was nothing unusual? He arranged his own work as he pleased?"

"Yes, I never interfered unless I wanted something special. He got through everything if you left him to it. He could be awkward if you tried to give him orders."

"So it was nothing surprising if he was missing from round the church for a couple of days or so in mid-week. He fitted in his gardening jobs for Miss Rachel as he thought best. And it looks as if he did go down to Treverra Place that same day, after he left the churchyard. Anyhow, the next we hear of him is there. About four o'clock he brought into the house a basket of plums he'd picked, told Miss Rachel he couldn't stay longer on the job then, but he'd come in next day and get in all the plums and apricots for bottling. Then he left. She saw him start down the drive. And so far that's the last we do know of him, until he turned up this morning in Treverra's coffin. According to the doctor's preliminary estimate, he was dead probably before nine o'clock, Wednesday night. Well, gentlemen, that's how it stands. Has anyone got anything to add? No second thoughts?"

"Yes," said Sam Shubrough, and: "Yes," said Simon at the same moment. They looked briefly at each other, and Simon waved a hand: "After you!"

" I've got a key," said Sam modestly. " One that belongs to that vault. I never bothered to mention it, because it wasn't needed, Miss Rachel was providing the one for official use. But it's plain now that you need to know about all the ways there are of getting in there, since somebody did get in and dump a body. So that's it. It's the only other key I *know* of, and I've got it. I'll turn it in if you want to have it in your own hands."

Hewitt closed his notebook with a movement of terrible forbearance. " Oh, you have a key. Well, that's helpful, at any rate. Would you mind telling us how you got it in the first place?"

" Not a bit. When I was a kid, St. Nectan's was our favourite playground. I found the key, once when we dug our way into the church for some game or other. It was down in the sand, under a nail on the wall, where I take it it used to hang. The wire on the bow was frayed through. I brought it home and cleaned it up, and it didn't take me long to find out it fitted the Treverra vault. We were a bit scared of going in," said Sam, smiling broadly under cover of his whiskers, " but sometimes we did. I've had the key ever since. It's in a bunch on a nail in my shed right now."

" Where, I take it, anyone could get at it? Do you keep the shed locked, even?"

" No, there's nothing special in it, and anyhow, we don't lock things, you know that. So I suppose anyone could get at it. But he'd have to know it was there, or else have an extraordinary stroke of luck, happening on it and finding out where it fitted. Do you want me to turn it in? I'll go and get it right now, if you've finished with me for the moment."

" If you'll be so good." And there were not now, and there never would be hereafter, any awkward questions about how, and how often, that key had been used. Hewitt was after a murderer, he was not going to be side-tracked. Sam rose and left the conference with only one bright, backward glance in Simon's direction.

"Now, Mr. Towne, you were going to add something, too?"

"Yes, I was. I didn't think much of it at the time—I don't now, for that matter—but you know all the talk there was when I first let it get round that I meant to open the Treverra tomb? A lot of people went off at half-cock, as usual, about the attempt being irreverent and blasphemous, about how a curse would fall on us, and so on. You must have heard it. Then when we made it known that it was a serious project, and the bishop had given permission, and Miss Rachel was positively egging us on, then all the fuss died down. All but this chap Trethuan. Well, of course, he was the verger, and I made allowances for certain prejudices, but he did begin to be a bit of a nuisance. He took every occasion he could to buttonhole me and try to persuade me to drop it. At first he just denounced it as ungodly, and said there'd be a judgment if we went ahead. Then he began to get threatening. I listened politely at first and made soothing noises, but I got tired of it finally and gave him the brush-off. But he didn't give up. He got more urgent."

"And was that what he spoke to you about on Wednesday," asked Hewitt, "when you came away from the vicarage?"

"It was all he ever spoke to me about. He saw me coming through the churchyard, and he came and stood right in the path, blocking the way, with the scythe in his hand. Something between Father Time and Holbein's 'Death'," said Simon wryly, "that long, bony man with his lantern face, clutching a scythe and pronouncing doom."

"Did he actually threaten you?"

"Physical threats? Not exactly. Just hints that I should regret it if I went ahead. But he did seem desperately disturbed about the whole thing, as if it was a matter of life and death to him."

"And what did you say to him?"

"Told him to do his worst, of course. Bring on your lightnings, I said, and pushed past him and left him standing there."

"By the Vicar's account," said Hewitt sharply, "he didn't stand there long. He didn't, by any chance, *follow* you to Treverra Place? He turned up there shortly afterwards."

"If he did, I never looked back to see. I didn't see him at the Place, either, I didn't know he was there. I spent the next hour or so with Miss Rachel, sitting talking in the garden. So it must have been after I left that he took his plums into the house and talked to her. I left around four o'clock, I suppose."

"You didn't say anything about Trethuan's queer behaviour to the old lady?"

"No, why should I? Oh, because it was her pet project—no, I didn't. I'd forgotten all about him by then, and anyhow, why bother Miss Rachel with it? We weren't even talking about Treverra that day, only about personal things."

"And after you left?"

"I hadn't brought the car out that day. I walked down into Maymouth for some cigarettes, and then took my time walking back over the Dragon's neck on my way home to Pentarno to tea. And that's when I came upon George's boy and our Paddy, down on the Pentarno beach. I saw them from the road and ran down to them. Dominic had just hauled Paddy out of the sea. And that reminds me," he said, stricken, " of why he said he went out so far. He said he'd seen a man in the sea."

"A man in the sea?" Hewitt's head jerked up smartly at that. "This is the first I've heard of any man in the sea."

"We didn't believe there ever was one. But, my God, now I'm beginning to wonder. It's like this, you see. There were these two boys, and it seemed Dominic had seen Paddy swimming dangerously far out off the point, and felt he ought to go and bring him in. But when he did, Paddy up and swore he thought he'd seen a body going out with the tide, and was trying to reach him. Dom and I went in again to see if we could see anything of him, but never a sign. Neither of us thought there was anything in it. But now—if Trethuan really drowned in the sea, as it seems he probably did——"

"About what time would that be?"

"Past five, maybe as late as half past, or even a little later. *Could* it have been? As early as that?"

"And only young Paddy actually claims he saw anything?"

"Even he wasn't positive. But he was worried. I promised I'd notify the coastguard, just to satisfy him, and I clean forgot. Not believing in it, you see, and then there was no report of anyone missing. I wish now I'd taken it more seriously."

Hewitt looked at Tim. "We'd better get hold of your boy, Mr. Rossall, and let him tell his own story. There may be nothing in it, but we can't afford to miss anything."

"I'll call him and tell him to bike over here. He'll come like a bird."

"Do. And maybe we'd better get your boy, too, Mr. Felse. He was on the scene before Mr. Towne arrived, there just may be something he can tell us." He handed the telephone across his desk, and Tim dialled his own number.

And thus began the great hunt for Paddy Rossall.

: :   : :

"No, he isn't," said Phil. "He didn't come home to lunch. I took it for granted he'd sneaked round to the dunes to watch your operations from a distance, since you wouldn't let him in on the ground floor. Maybe he cadged a lunch with Aunt Rachel. Try there. I'm waiting for those apricots, the monkey!" She added at the last moment, with the first faint and distant hint of anxiety in her voice : "Call me back if you find him, Tim, won't you?"

: :   : :

"No, he isn't," said Miss Rachel, with some asperity because of her own irrepressible conscience. "Tamsin took a snack out to him about half past eleven, and he'd already filled his basket and gone. Naturally I took it he'd taken them home to Phil. Oh—and he hasn't been near the church, either? He'd want to keep out of sight, of course. Well, don't fuss over him, Tim, that's fatal. He'll come home when he's hungry."

She replaced the receiver with unnecessary violence, and found Tamsin studying her very narrowly across the desk.

"I gather Paddy didn't go home."

"No, he didn't. You said yourself where he'd most likely be," snapped Miss Rachel.

"I know I did, but it seems he isn't. And I didn't know, when I published my estimate, what you'd been saying to him—did I?"

"You still don't," pointed out Miss Rachel, all the more maliciously for the alarm she couldn't quite allay, and wouldn't acknowledge. "He'll come home when he's got everyone nicely worried, that's what he's after. I'm not going to fall for that, if you're stupid enough to buy it. Children are born blackmailers."

He was perfectly all right, of course. He was simply hiding somewhere and sulking, and gloating over the uneasiness he was causing everyone. Well, it wasn't going to work. He'd run away once, as a very small boy—like many another before him, in dudgeon over some fancied injustice. But he'd come home fast enough when it began to rain. Children are realists; they know which side their bread's buttered.

::   ::

"No, he isn't," said Dominic, surprised. "Have you got Dad there? No, not to worry, only we heard the rumours that are running round, and we couldn't help wondering. But we haven't seen anything of Paddy. Yes, of course I'll come, like a shot. Well, I've been out there on the Head part of the morning, it *is* like a grandstand, but I haven't seen hide or hair of Paddy. Look, suppose I scout round now, before I come down, and see if I can find out anything? No, there's hardly anybody hanging about round the church now, only a handful of people who were late coming, but I'll have a look there, too. Sure, I'll be down as soon as I can make it."

::   ::

"He isn't anywhere," said Tim, banging down the receiver for the tenth time. Dominic was already with them by then, with a negative report and a curiosity that positively hurt him, though he was containing it manfully. "That's all his closest friends crossed off. And he hasn't had anything to eat! I don't like it."

Hewitt didn't like it, either. His solid face, conditioned to the suppression of all feeling except the deceptive pessimism he used for business purposes, was letting anxiety through like a slow leak.

"He wouldn't go off anywhere out of town without telling anyone. He isn't irresponsible. It isn't that he'd do anything harebrained. But anyone can have an accident."

"I'm wondering," said Hewitt heavily, "if he saw something else, when he saw—or thought he saw—that body in the water. Maybe without at all realising the significance of what he was seeing. I'm wondering if he saw *someone* else, say up on the Head above the rocks, just at the crucial moment. Or whether somebody who was up there may *think* Paddy saw him, even if he didn't."

"You don't think he could be in danger?" asked Tim, shaken and pale.

"I'd have said no, up to this noon. But now it's all over this town that Trethuan's body has turned up, and the hunt's on. Whoever killed him will be pretty desperate now to remove anyone who may—even may—have noticed and recognised him, and may blurt out to the police what he knows."

"Then we've got to find Paddy, quickly. My God, if anything happened to him——"

"Nothing will happen to him," protested Simon strongly. "He'll turn up soon, safe and sound, and with a perfectly simple explanation, you see if he doesn't."

But Hewitt was already on his feet, and reaching for the telephone. "I'd rather not wait, Mr. Towne. What was he wearing this morning? Oh, Blakey, I want every man we can spare, we've got a full-scale hunt on our hands. We've lost a boy—young Paddy Rossall, most of our fellows will know him on sight. Missing with a bike, since this morning. Yes, we need everybody."

"Well, if it's like that, you've got a handful of volunteers right here," said Simon, solid and calm at Tim's shoulder. "You're the boss, where do we start?"

: :   : :

Tamsin turned from her uneasy pacing along the range of the library windows, and marched through the doorway into Miss Rachel's sitting-room. The old lady looked up with a face resolutely complacent, and told herself for the twentieth time that day that young people nowadays had no stamina. No wonder all modern children were spoiled.

"They still haven't found him," said Tamsin. "I'm sick of this, I'm going down to help look for him."

"You're going to do nothing of the sort. Don't be foolish. His parents are bad enough, there's no need for you to start. The boy is where he went of his own will, you may be absolutely sure, and he'll turn up when it suits him. When he's demoralised everybody so much that he needn't fear reprisals. Not before!"

"You," said Tamsin forcefully, "are a heartless old woman, that's what you are. I wish you'd tell me what you did to him this morning. I know there's something."

"What I did to him, indeed! Don't be impertinent! I'm the old woman who pays your salary, at any rate," said Miss Rachel tartly, because no matter how firmly she held the door, the demons were getting through it. "You'd better remember that, miss. I hate dining alone, and you know it. And I haven't had my game of chess. So stop being melodramatic, and get the board."

"You'll have to make do with patience," said Tamsin. "I shan't be here."

Miss Rachel called after her towards the door, in high indignation. "If you go, you needn't bother to come back."

"Good-bye, then," said Tamsin pleasantly, and closed the door after her without even a slam.

Miss Rachel, left alone, was astonished and annoyed to find herself crying.

CHAPTER V

FRIDAY EVENING

THE TIDE WAS two hours past the full, and it was getting dark. The cauldron off the point was just going off the boil, slivers of slate-grey pebbly beach showed between the fangs of the Dragon, rimmed with scummy foam. The Dragon's Hole, which pierced clean through the headland near its narrowest point, and acted as a spectacular blow-hole as the tide streamed in to its highest, was merely breathing spume now in a desultory manner, as though the Dragon was falling asleep. Soon the dripping crown of the arched entrance would heave clear of the water, and the level would sink magically fast, to leave the whole rocky gateway clear. At low tide you could clamber and walk right through it, and emerge in the snaky little haven on the Pentarno side. Certain regions of the complex of caverns inside were always above water, but for three hours before and after high tide both entrances were submerged.

They were all in the hunt by then. Phil had driven in from the farm in the Mini, pale and strained and violently silent, matched herself with the first partner who happened to come in with his periodical, and negative report, and gone off with him to scour the most distant of the Maymouth beaches. Fate dealt her George, for which she was grateful, because that compelled her to behave sensibly and contain her terrors; she couldn't have borne to be with Tim just then, to double his anguish and her own.

Bunty had come down from the hotel, determined not to be left out, workmanlike in slacks and a windjacket, and was quartering the country fringes of Maymouth with

the Vicar, in case Paddy had had a fall or a crash somewhere on his intended way home. There were precipitous
lanes he might have chosen to use, to vary the monotony of
his journey, and a cyclist can come to grief on even the
quietest of roads, given a little carelessness or a too-optim-
istic local driver who assumes no one uses these by-ways
but himself. Everyone who was at all intimate with the boy
had been telephoned and asked to keep in touch. What
more could they do but just look everywhere, and go on
looking?

Tamsin and Dominic had worked their way the length
of the harbour, down on the mud, following up the receding
tide, and come empty-handed to the remotest rocks under
the wall, where ashlar gave way to granite and shale, and
the jagged scales of the Dragon leaned over them. The sea
still lipped the cliffs here, they could go no farther as yet.
They turned inland, hugging the cliff wall, winding in and
out of its many razor-edged alcoves, and the crying of the
subsiding waves followed them mournfully. They were
drenched with spray and very muddy. Dominic had the
torch, and sometimes turned to empty its light carefully
before her feet in the rough places, and give her a hand.
She knew every inch of this shore, but she took the hand,
just the same. They were both glad of the touch. This
had been going on for such a long time now, and where can
you lose a sensible, responsible boy of fifteen, where, at
least, that hadn't already been searched? Except in the
sea! They wouldn't think that, they couldn't, it was un-
thinkable. Paddy was strong, shrewd and capable, and
knew his native coast. He was alive, he must be alive.

They climbed slowly out of the pebbly fringes of the
sea, towards where the first steep path plunged down from
the Dragon's Head. A surging rush of air was all the warning they had. They sprang apart before the hurtling on-
slaught of something that came bounding down the slope,
flashed between them, and was dragged to a noisy stop
by a toe horribly scoring the turf. Small, invisible things
hopped and rolled under their feet. A voice, anxious, urgent
and low, panted: " Tam, is that you?"

Stumbling and slipping on the rolling missiles, Tamsin groped for a tweed sleeve. Dominic turned the torch, and Simon's face started out of the dark, abrupt in black and white, strained to steel-sharpness, for once utterly bereft of its light, world-weary smile.

"Simon, for God's sake! What are you trying to do, kill yourself? Fancy riding a bicycle down——"

Tamsin stopped, swallowed, drew breath hard and was silent. The light of the torch passed briefly over the frame of the bicycle, the carrier on the front, the basket spilling small oval fruit. They had no colour by this light, but Tamsin knew them for apricots. She whispered, "Where did you find it?"

"In the gorse, up by the cliff path there. Put down quite carefully, the basket lifted out. Near the edge," said Simon, low-voiced and ashen-faced. "Not exactly hidden. Laid down out of the way."

"He did it himself?"

"I think so. I hope so. I'm going to turn it in at once, in case it can tell us anything."

"*Where* along the path?" she demanded intently. Her voice had lost its reserve in Simon's presence, and its sting, too, as his face had lost its assured sophistication. It was as if they had never bumped into each other without masks before, and now that they had, they couldn't even see each other.

"Farther out. Over the blow-hole, about. Have you been down there?"

"We couldn't yet, not so far. It's going out fast now, though, we'll follow on down."

"Do, Tam, please. I'll be with you as soon as I can."

"Do you think he could have fallen?" she asked, desperately quietly.

"I don't know. I won't think so. I—Oh, Tam!" said Simon suddenly, his voice almost inaudible, and caught at her hand for a moment; and instantly pulled away from her, climbed unsteadily on to the bicycle that was too small for him, and wobbled away recklessly across the bumpy waste of turf to the road and the town. Soiled and dishevelled and faintly ridiculous, and for once wholly, passionately intent upon someone other than himself, without a thought for the preservation of his image or his legend.

Dominic switched off the torch; and after a moment he put an arm delicately but quite confidently about Tamsin, and turned her towards the sea.

: :   : :

They followed the receding tide down the beach yard by yard, ranging along the edge of the water and coasting round into every new complexity of the cliff wall, which ran down here in striated, shaly strata into the litter of flat, blue pebbles and eroded shell. A certain amount of lambent light showed along the breaking foam, and gleamed from the streaming rocks, and their torch, a thin pencil in the dark, probed the corners where even the starlight could not reach.

"That *was* Simon?" said Tamsin suddenly, all the old obduracy back in her voice.

"Well, that's what you called him," said Dominic cautiously.

"Thanks. Just making sure. It's the first time I ever saw him when he didn't have an imaginary mirror in front of him. He must be really fond of Paddy."

"He is," said Dominic.

"Do I detect a note of reproof in your voice, Mr. Felse?"

He said nothing. What was the good? Only a tiny corner of her mind fretted at the memory of Simon off his guard, and that was to make their one overwhelming anxiety bearable, like pinching yourself to take your mind off a hideous toothache. Any serious thinking she was going to do about it would be done later, in repose, when, please God, they'd have Paddy Rossall safe in bed, and Simon restored to his old image. And then he'd start rubbing her up the wrong way all over again.

"You'll notice," she said perversely, her shoes slipping in the weedy crevices of the rock, "he never asks me to marry him when there might be the slightest fear of me saying yes." She slithered into the edge of an invisible pool, and Dominic caught her by the arm and drew her back on to safe ground.

" All right?"

" Fine! Just a shoe-full of sea. It can't make me any wetter." She held on to him for a moment, steadying herself. Her hands were very cold. He saw her face close to him, feathers of wet hair plastered to her cheek, her eyes sombre and wretched. " Dom—we shall find him, shan't we?"

" Yes," he said, very firmly. " He's a sensible kid, I don't believe he'd let anyone creep up on him, and I don't believe he'd do anything daft himself." Which from eighteen to fifteen, when Tamsin came to think of it, was pretty generous, but he sounded as if he really meant it. " He'll be found intact," said Dominic strenuously, " and with any luck, we shall be the ones to find him. So hang on, and let's have a look round the next corner."

They had looked round a good many by then, with their hearts in their mouths at every turning, but so far there'd been no slight, tumbled body under the cliffs, and nothing washing about in the edge of the retreating waves but casual weed.

" Yes," she said docilely. And after a moment, very quietly at his shoulder: " You're a nice boy, Dominic Felse, I like you."

" Good! I like you, too, I like you a lot. There, you see, nothing!" He couldn't help reflecting, as soon as it was out, that nothing was a pretty poor return for all their hunting, and a pretty lame reassurance for Paddy's mother. But it was all they had, and it was better than the wrong thing, at any rate.

The sea sighed away from them, down the more steeply tilted shingle. They stood close under the overhang of the cliff, on a washed and empty shore, and right above their heads must be the necklace of the lofty path that circled the Dragon's Head, and the scattered hollows of gorse where Simon had found the bicycle. The waters had left the arched entrance of the cave now, it stood tamed and dark above a faint glimmer of salt puddles penned among the boulders.

They halted for only a second, contemplating it together.

"He wouldn't," said Tamsin, "would he?"

"Not without a reason, but he may have had a reason, how do we know?"

"But he knows the tides, he wouldn't let himself get caught."

"Something may have happened that didn't leave him any choice. Anyhow, we're not leaving anything out."

"Careful, then," she cautioned, drawing him to the right, to the landward side of the thin channel of water that lay prisoned among the pebbles in the cavern's mouth. "This side's the smoothest going. And look out, there are holes."

Dominic fell into one at that moment, cold salt water gripped him to the knees, and the chilling shock surprised a muted yell out of him. Deep in the blackness beyond the beam of the torch, echo took the shout and volleyed it back to him redoubled.

"Dom!" Tamsin caught at his arm. "Did you hear that?"

Floundering out of the crevices on slippery oblique rock, he supposed that she was as startled by the force and complexity of the echo as he had been, and merely went on scrambling noisily up to safer ground. "Hear it? I started it. It wasn't that good an imitation——"

"No—listen!" She shook him impatiently, and he froze into obedient silence, straining his ears.

Nothing at first, not a sound; then they were aware of the ceaseless, soft, universal sound of the dripping of sea water from every jutting point of the stone ceiling above them and the contorted walls around, and the soft, busy flowing of a dozen rivulets draining down between the pebbles into the central channel behind them. The place was full of the sounds of water, but empty of the sounds of men.

"But it wasn't all echo. I'm sure!"

Almost fearfully, Dominic called upward into the invisible spaces of the cave: "Paddy?"

The call came eddying back to him from a dozen projections he could not see, repeated in a dozen hopeful, fearful inflections, ricocheting away into silence. Then a last faint and distant sound, out of turn, out of key, started a weak reverberation away on their right.

"There! Hear that? There *is* someone!"

But Dominic was already scrambling wildly up the rattling scree of sand and gravel and shell, the pencil of wavering light wincing away from rocks and water-drips before him, clawing his way up towards the drier reaches of the cave. He stretched out a hand to her and dragged her after him. Stumbling, slipping, panting, they climbed inland; and somewhere ahead of them, distant and faint but drawing nearer, unmistakable sounds of someone else's stumbling, slipping, panting progress came down to meet them.

Into the beam of the torch blundered Paddy Rossall, wiping his dirty face hastily with an even dirtier hand; pallid, wet, and shivering with cold, but alive, intact and alone.

::   ::

"You don't mind," said Phil, turning in at the drive of Treverra Place, "if we call in here? I don't know that it will do any good, but I just thought, while we're so near— She might remember *something* he said, anything that will give us the faintest clue. I know we've asked the same questions already, but it's worth one more try. Oh, George, my poor little boy! I wish I hadn't said no to him. I wish I'd let him go with Tim and Simon—at least he'd have been safe with them."

It was the most she had said in all the hours they had hunted together. As long as there'd been more places to search, more possible people to contact, Phil had been a silent, ferocious force of nature sweeping all before her. Only now, when they had almost exhausted the possibilities, was the edge of desperation audible in her voice, and the shadow of breakdown a perceptible cloud over her face.

Miss Rachel was sitting over the fire in her sitting-room, huddled like a broody bird, with her solitary dinner untouched on a little table beside her. She stiffened her old spine and snapped the imperious lights on again in her eyes when Phil stalked in with George at her elbow, but she knew her back was against the wall.

"Aunt Rachel, didn't he say *anything* about where he was going? There must have been something. You did see him yourself, didn't you? Well, what *did* he say? I *know* we're snatching at crumbs. Damn it, crumbs is all we've got."

"Yes, I talked to him, certainly." Miss Rachel looked smaller than usual, but fiercer. Attack is the best defence. "What passed between Paddy and me can't possibly have anything to do with any danger to him. But it may—I say *may*—account for his naughtiness in staying away like this. If you ask me, that's all it is, and you are just playing into his hands. I was justified in being cross with him. He was exceedingly impertinent and very disobedient, and it was high time someone took steps to bring him to a more chastened frame of mind."

Quivering and aghast, Phil demanded : "But what— for God's sake, Aunt Rachel, what *did* you do to him?"

She couldn't stall any longer, it would only make it worse when it did come out. And besides, she was lonely and frightened and she wanted Paddy back, impertinent or not, disobedient or not, she just wanted him. So somebody had to find him for her.

"It's too much to hope that you'll approve, of course, but I was concerned only for you and Tim, and for the child's own well-being. I told him what he should have been told as soon as he was old enough to understand— that he has to thank you and Tim for taking him in and giving him a good home and the love of good parents, when his own father wanted to get rid of him. I told him he was adopted, and that he should consider how much he owed to you, and try to behave better to you in future, not take everything for granted as he does. That's what I told him, and you'll have reason to thank me for it yet."

Stricken, Phil stood clinging to the back of a chair as to the rocking remnants of her world. "Aunt Rachel! You couldn't! You *couldn't* be so cruel!"

"Cruel, nonsense! It was high time he was told, you'd have had to do it in the end. I don't believe it's done him one jot of harm, either, so——"

"No *harm*!" Groping through the blankness of her misery, Phil arrived at a positive and tonic fury. Her cheeks flushed scarlet, and paled again to a pinched and frightening whiteness. "No *harm*! You drive that poor boy away with the bottom knocked out of his world, not knowing who or what he is, and you say you've done him no *harm*!"

"It means we're probably all wrong about his being in danger from our murderer," pointed out George quickly, with a gentling hand on her arm. "He's shocked and hurt and wretched, he wants to hide, that's all understandable. But it means he's probably staying away of his own will, and when he's come to terms with it he'll come home. It isn't as bad as what we were afraid of."

"It is, George, it's almost worse. He'll be in such a state he might do *anything*." She turned frantically upon Miss Rachel, who was backed into her great chair with hackles erect, ready for a fight. "How would *you* feel, you wicked old woman, if you suddenly found you weren't who you thought you were, and your parents weren't your parents, and everything you had was borrowed? Even your identity?" She gripped the edge of the table, and demanded urgently: "Did you tell him *who* he was? But you couldn't —we never told you, thank God, so you didn't know."

"Oh, yes, my dear Phil, I did know. His father told me himself—right here in the garden, no longer ago than Wednesday afternoon. He told me quite a lot. But I didn't tell Paddy. I don't have to tell everything I know." She drew breath before Phil could ride over her again, and pursued belligerently: "But *you'd* better. Oh, I know, Simon thinks he can twist me round his finger. Maybe I like it that way. But don't think I've got any illusions about him. I like him very much, but sooner or later he'll make a bid for what he wants. And if you haven't noticed that he's beginning to want Paddy, very much indeed, you'd better wake up, quickly."

George, whose experience in breaking up fights between women was still somewhat inadequate to such a situation as this, felt profound gratitude to the telephone for ringing just then. It gave him something to do, more constructive than listening to family secrets it would be his duty promptly to forget again, and it distracted the attention of both the embattled females. He picked up the receiver thankfully.

"Treverra Place. This is George Felse. Oh, yes— yes, she's here. Phil, it's Tamsin Holt for you."

Phil clutched the receiver convulsively, afraid to hope. "Tamsin, what is it? Have you—*You have*! Thank God! He's all right?"

Her knees gave under her, she was suddenly limp as silk, and George slid a chair under her and eased her into it.

"*He's all right*! They've found him. In the Dragon's Hole. The tide caught him inside there. Aunt Rachel, it's all right! They've found him—Tamsin and Dominic. I don't care now, nothing else matters. I don't care what you told him, he's all right. Tam—we're on our way down, we'll meet you. Take care of him! Don't you let him out of your sight again. The little *demon*! Honestly, I'll murder him! You're *sure* he isn't hurt? God bless you, Tam! We're on our way."

She let the receiver slip nervelessly down into its cradle. She was in tears, and trembling. "George, can you drive a Mini? I—don't think I'm capable—Oh, George, *I want Tim*!"

George got her to her feet and out to the car. No one had even a glance to spare for Miss Rachel, braced and defensive in her high-backed chair.

As soon as they were out of the doorway she hopped suddenly out of her sanctuary behind the cold dinner-tray, and danced the length of the room and the library, like an agile girl, until her piled grey hair came down round her shoulders, and she was out of breath. Then, having carefully reassembled her magnificent coiffure and her even

more magnificent personal assurance, she rang the bell for
Alice, and demanded food.

::   ::

On their way down through the town they picked up Tim.
Phil clung to him in the back seat, pouring out the best
and the worst of the news, and swinging breathlessly between rage and joy. Tim held her in his arms and shook
with the vehemence of her trembling, and implored her
first, and then ordered her, just as ineffectively, to be calm
and matter-of-fact, and take the whole thing easily. Hadn't
they agreed from the beginning that with a child not your
own you must take nothing for granted, that you had to
exercise twice as much care and self-control as natural
parents, and earn every morsel of your gift-son's affection?
Restraint, no too greedy love, no too lavish indulgences
and no too exacting demands, that was the way. If she
let herself go now, she'd push the boy right over the edge,
and break something.

"Here they are," said George at the wheel, and drew
the Mini in to the kerb just below the square, the dilapidated
trio before them caught and dazzled in its lights. A slim,
taut, brittle figure toiled up the hill between two muddy
supporters just recognisable as Tamsin and Dominic. He
had been drooping badly a moment before, but now he
was braced to meet them. The moment was on top of him;
he wasn't ready, but he never would be ready, it might as
well happen and get it over. A pale, grime-streaked face
stared, all enormous, shocked eyes. Phil lunged for the door-
handle and was half out of the car before it came to a
halt.

"Phil, you must be *calm*——"

"To hell with being calm!" shouted Phil, in a splendid
flare of wrathful joy, and hurled herself upon her stray in
a flurry of abuse, endearments and reproaches.

Paddy's parent problem was swept away in the warm,
sweet hurricane. After all, he didn't have to make any
decisions about how to behave, he didn't have to do anything at all. The meeting he had been dreading was taken
clean out of his hands. He was plucked from between

his henchmen, hugged, shaken, even he seemed to remember afterwards with respect and astonishment, slapped, a thing he couldn't remember ever having happened to him before in his life. Tim snatched him from Phil to feel him all over, swear at him heartily, strip him of his wet and filthy sweater, and bundle him into a warm, dry sportscoat much too big for him. He could hardly get a word in edgeways, all he managed was: "I'm sorry!" and: "I didn't mean to!" and : "I couldn't help it!" at intervals. And he had been shrinking from the thought of moderated voices and careful handling, into which he would inevitably have read all sorts of reservations! There weren't any moderated voices round here, he couldn't hear himself think; and the way he was being handled, he was going to start coming to pieces shortly. This sort of thing there was no mistaking. He was loved, all right. She was frantic about him, and Dad wasn't much better. This, he thought, hustled and scolded and abused and caressed into dazed silence, this is *exactly* how parents behave.

"Into that car," ordered Tim, growing grimmer by the minute now that he had satisfied himself that he had his son back with hardly a scratch on him. "You're going to apologise to Mr. Hewitt for all the trouble you've caused everybody, and you'd better make it good." And when he had him penned into the back seat, with Phil to cushion him comfortably, he had to rummage out the old car rug and tuck him into it like a cocoon, and all to go the two hundred yards to the police station.

The rest of the evening always remained to him a crazy confusion, from which fleeting remarks emerged at times to tickle his memory. The one overwhelming thing about it was that all of it, every bit, was good, better than anything had ever been before, or perhaps ever would be again. To have happiness and know that you have it, and know how wonderful it is to know it, that's almost too much for any one day.

He was bundled into the warmth and light of the police station, blinking and exhausted, and made his apologies with quite unexpected grace, out of the fullness of his own plenty. He said thank you to everyone who had gathered there from the great boy-hunt, and requested that his thanks be conveyed to all those who were not there to hear for themselves. Hewitt received the offering with considerable complacency, out of pure relief, but maintained a solemn face.

"Don't you think you've heard the last of it, young feller-me-lad. Your next six months' pocket-money's going to be needed to pay for police shoe-leather. I'll be sending you in a bill." He grinned at Tim over the tow-coloured head that was beginning to be unconscionably heavy. "Take him home, clean him up and put him to bed, Mr. Rossall. I'll talk to him in the morning, he's out on his feet now."

He remembered looking round a whole ring of faces when he said good-night. Mr. Felse was there with his wife, Tamsin was there, and Dominic, and the Vicar, and Uncle Simon. Uncle Simon was looking at him in an odd sort of way, smiling, but without the sparkle, and twice as hard as usual. And he didn't come with them. Why didn't he? Oh, yes, of course, he probably had his own car here, so he had to drive it home. But it didn't look as if that was in his mind, somehow, when he shook his head at Dad, with that odd, rueful smile on his face, and said: "No, I'll follow you down later, old boy. This is a family special."

That reminded Paddy of how this extraordinary day had started. There were things he still had to know about himself, but somehow all the urgency was already gone. In the back seat of the car, rolled up again snugly in the rug, with Phil's arm round him, and Phil's shoulder comfortable and comforting under his cheek, he drowsed gloriously, too tired to know anything clearly except the one wonderful, all-pervading fact that it was all right. That everything was all right, because his belonging to them was everything.

And whoever he might have belonged to in the beginning, he was certainly theirs now. Heaven help anyone who tried to take him away from them, or them from him!

　　: :　　　　　　　: :

"I'm glad you know I know," he said out of his pillows, bathed, fed, warmed and cosseted, and drowning in a delicious, sleepy happiness. "It did come as a bit of a shock at first, that's why I sheered off from Aunt Rachel's without telling anybody. I wasn't trying to frighten anyone, or run away from home, or anything daft, like that. Honestly! I'm not such a clot."

"I should hope not," said Tim.

"No, but I was afraid you might think—I just felt shaken up, and not wanting to see anybody, or be talked to. You know! I started for home, and then I couldn't face it, not until I'd had time to think. I went up on the Head, instead, but it was *swarming*. People everywhere. I just ditched the bike, and nipped down the cliff path and into the cave, where I knew I could be quiet. Just till I got a bit more used to it, that's all. But then some kids came in, playing, and I backed up as far as I could, to get out of their way."

Having, thought Phil, who had not failed to distinguish the tear-marks from the general stains of sea-water and cave-grime, an entirely visible and possibly temporarily uncontrollable distress to hide by then.

"Never mind now, darling, you go to sleep. There's time for all that to-morrow. You're home, and that's all that matters."

"Yes, but I just wanted you to know I wasn't sulking, or anything childish like that. It was just by accident I happened to find this passage in the top end of the cave. Only a low sort of hole, you have to crawl through it on hands and knees. I was backed up into this corner, and I shoved my shoulder through it in the dark. It goes a long way. That's how I lost time, having to be careful because of not having a light. In the end I did call it a day and decide to come back some other time with a torch, but what with not being able to see my watch, and forgetting because I was interested, by the time I crawled back through the hole I'd had it. The water was almost up to the top of the cave mouth, and I didn't dare dive for it, it was too rough. I had to lie up and wait, there wasn't anything else to do." He looked up with the remembered terror suddenly brilliant in his eyes, squarely into Tim's face. "I was scared green," he said.

"So would I have been. Even knowing that the top part of the Hole's above high water, I'd still have been scared."

"And even there you get a bit battered. And deafened! I couldn't wait to get out, it seemed for ever. I couldn't tell what time it was, you see, I just had to follow the water down, and you have to be super-cautious feeling your way in the dark. But I was on my way out as fast as I dared when they came and found me."

Phil turned the shaded light away from her own face, for fear he should see his ordeal reflected there all too plainly, stroked the fuzz of fair hair back from his forehead, and said: "Yes, well, it's all over now. You just forget it and go to sleep."

"Yes—all right, I will. I just wanted you to know how it was. I'm sorry I caused everybody so much trouble." Half asleep and off his guard, he said with shattering simplicity: "I was just so miserable I didn't know what to do."

Tim hooked a large right fist to the angle of his son's jaw, and rolled the fair head gently on the pillow till a shamefaced grin came through.

"Did you say you weren't a clot? You could have fooled me! Sure you know now where you live?" The drowsy head nodded; the grin had a curious but happy shyness. "And what time the tide comes in? All right, then, you sleep it off. If you want anything we'll be around." He rose, rolled Paddy over in the bed, and smacked the slight hummock of his rump under the clothes. "Good-night, son!"

"Good-night, Dad!"

All the years they'd been saying exactly the same words, and they'd never meant so much before!

Phil kissed the spot where the blonde hair grew to a slight point on the smooth forehead, and was following Tim from the room when a small, self-conscious voice behind her said: "Mummy!"

The tone of it tugged her back to him in a hurry. He hadn't said it without thought, it had a ceremonial solemnity. She stooped over him, and he pushed away the bed-clothes suddenly and reached up his arms for her, burrowing his face thankfully into the hollow of her neck.

"Just making sure," he said in a muffled whisper. "You *are*, aren't you?"

"Yes, I am, Patrick Rossall, and don't you dare forget it."

::   ::

She gathered up his clothes when she left the room. The flannels would have to go straight to the cleaners. She sat down on the rug beside Tim, and extracted from the pockets, smiling over them with a ridiculous tenderness because they were small projections of Paddy's personality, one exceedingly grubby handkerchief, sticky with sea-water, a ball pen down to its last inch, the end chewed, two or three foreign stamps, a used bus ticket, one dilapidated toffee, and a few coins, which she stacked carefully on the arm of Tim's chair.

"He's all right, isn't he?" said Tim, ears pricked for any sound from upstairs.

"Yes, he's all right." Her smile was heavy, maternal and assured. "Don't worry about Paddy. Tim, I'm glad! I'm glad she told him. It's a once-only. He knows now."

"He's a nice kid," said Tim. He took up the little pile of coins to play with, because they were Paddy's. "Look, a brand-new halfpenny." He looked again, and froze. "It isn't, though! What is it? Phil, look! It isn't copper. It looks like gold!"

She dropped the crumpled, dirty flannels, and held out her hand curiously for the coin. It lay demurely in her palm, showing a thick-necked female profile, with a curled lock of hair draped over one plump shoulder.

"Tim, it must be a guinea! Or a half-guinea—but it's too big, isn't it? ANNA DEI GRATIA. And VIGO underneath her portrait. What does that mean? There's a date on the other side, 1703. REG. MAG. BR. FR. et HIB." She looked up at Tim over her spread palm, open-mouthed. "Tim, where on earth did our Paddy get a Queen Anne guinea?"

CHAPTER VI

SATURDAY MORNING

PHIL LOOKED IN at Paddy's door as soon as she was up on
Saturday morning. The early sunlight came in softened
and dimmed through the drawn curtains, and the boy
lay curled comfortably, with cheek and nose burrowed
into his pillow, fast asleep. She looked at him with her
love like a warm, golden weight in her, and was drawing
back silently when a faint movement in the shadows of
one corner arrested her.

Simon was sitting in a chintz-covered chair, drawn back
where the light could not reach him. He was looking at
her by the time she saw him; but she knew very well that
until that moment he had been watching Paddy's sleep.
He looked as if he had been there half the night. Maybe
he had. He had his own key, and she hadn't heard him
come in.

Only a few days ago she would have stiffened in jealousy
and suspicion, willing him away, and stared her orders
unmistakably. Now she stood looking at him thoughtfully
and calmly, and in her heart she was sorry for him. It
was the first time she had ever achieved that. This morning
she was sorry for everybody who wasn't herself or Tim,
and hadn't got a son like Paddy; and sorriest of all for
Simon Towne, who had had one and lacked the sense to
hang on to him while he had him. She smiled, meeting his
tired and illusionless eyes. He got up very quietly, as
though she had warned him off, and followed her out of
the room and down the stairs.

"I'll grind the coffee," he offered, following her into
the kitchen. He was handier about the house than Tim,
and quieter. She supposed widowers of long experience—
nearly fifteen years now—easily might be. She began
preparing breakfast. Even the solid blue and white crockery

99

looked new, as if to-day everything began afresh. But not for Simon.

Not because she had the better of him, and knew it, but because he was a figure so much more appealing now that he was shaken and vulnerable and fit for sympathy, she had never liked him so much before. But you couldn't alter Simon, or teach him anything, just by liking him better. He would have to learn the hard way.

"Have you been to bed?" she asked, slicing bread.

"No. I brought the Land-Rover down with Paddy's bike aboard, and then fetched the car and went for a long ride. Then I came home and lay down for a bit, and had a bath. I hope I didn't disturb you when I came in?"

"No, I didn't hear you. How long have you been guarding Paddy's sleep?" She didn't sound either suspicious or resentful; he found that surprising, and for some reason it pricked a spring of resentment in him.

"I don't know. A couple of hours or so. I enjoy looking at him. Do you mind?"

"No, I'm glad. I enjoy looking at him, too." She came from the pantry with a bowl of eggs balanced on one hand, a jug of milk in the other. Simon left his grinding to take the eggs from her, and being so near, leaned impulsively and kissed her cheek, without apology or explanation. Phil smiled at him. "It's all right, Simon. I know what happened to you, when you were afraid Paddy was gone for good. But do you know what happened to him? A fifteen-year-old bubble burst, my dear, and we're none of us ever going to be the same again. Miss Rachel got annoyed because Paddy was cheeky to her, and because she thought he didn't appreciate his good home as he ought. So she told him he only enjoyed it on sufferance. He knows now that he——" She couldn't say: "He isn't ours," because it wouldn't be true; it would be more monstrously untrue now than it had ever been before. "He knows we adopted him. That's what happened to Paddy."

Simon put the eggs down very carefully on the kitchen table, and straightened up to turn upon her the gravest face, and the least concerned for the effect it might be producing upon the outside world, that she had ever seen him wear. After a long moment of quietness he asked in a voice that was avoiding strain with some care: "Did she tell him he was really mine?"

Phil smiled. He hadn't chosen the words as a challenge or a claim, in a sense he hadn't consciously chosen them at all, but they still indicated his implicit belief in their truth. "No, she didn't. But she told me she could have. After all this time, why *did* you tell her?"

"I don't know," he said honestly. "I suppose I simply wanted *somebody* to know, just so that I could talk about him and be understood. Preferably somebody who'd feel sorry for me, to tell the whole truth. But I never meant this to happen, Phil. I suppose it's because of what I told her that she had this thing in her mind, a stick all ready to beat him with when he offended her. I'm sorry! I never thought of anything like that."

"I know, I'm not blaming you."

"But since he knows so much—I don't know that I'd feel there was anything now to stop me from telling him the rest." He turned on the gas ring and put on the kettle with steady and leisurely movements. A fine spark of intent had kindled deep in his eyes, and that meant mischief. The faintest hint of the usual bold quirk twitched at the corner of his mouth, and again his face had a wayward acquisitiveness about it. Tamsin's hackles had risen at sight of that debonair and much-admired face with which he pursued his dearest objectives, but it hadn't taught him anything.

"You won't have to bother," said Phil. "I'll tell him myself."

"You?" He was surprised into a genuine laugh.

"I haven't much alternative now, have I? You must know very well that the first thing he's going to ask me, when he gets round to thinking about it seriously, is: Who am I? Of course I shall tell him."

She turned and looked at him sharply, and saw exactly what she had expected to see, the sleek glow of triumph

and speculation and hope warming his face into golden
confidence. She closed the oven door with a crisp slam.

"Look, Simon, wake up, while there's time. It isn't
going to do you any good, you know."

"Isn't it? Phil, you're positively inviting me to see what
I can do. Aren't you afraid I'll sneak him away from under
your nose even now? Don't you think I could?"

"I know you couldn't," she said steadily. "I don't
think you'd even try, if I begged you not to. But I'm
not begging you—am I? I don't have to, Simon, that's
why. You couldn't get him away from us now whatever
you did, fair or foul. You've had a long innings, charming
the birds from the trees, and getting golden apples to fall
into your lap whenever you smiled. You can't realise,
can you, that it isn't going to last for ever? The high days
are over, Simon, middle age is only just round another
corner or two. You'd better start settling for what you can
get, because the long holiday's running out fast. And
whatever you do, you won't get Paddy."

For a moment it seemed to her that his brightness had
grown sharp and brittle, and his eyes were staring at something he would rather not have seen. Then they took heart
and danced again.

"What will you bet me?" he said with soft deliberation.

Remembering the long years of friendship through which
Tim had followed him around patiently, picking up the
things Simon dropped and putting together the things
Simon broke, she wondered for a moment if her motives
were as pure as she would have liked. But if it was vengeful pleasure that was prompting her to invite him to his
downfall, why was this moment so sad, so strangely
the shadowy reverse of the serenity and joy that made this
morning a portent and a prodigy? And why should she
feel so much closer and kinder to him than she had ever
felt before?

"I should be betting you Paddy, shouldn't I?" she said,
gently and quietly. "What more do you want?"

: :   : :

Paddy opened his eyes and stretched delightedly, and then

remembered why everything felt and looked different to-day. Not necessarily better or worse, not yet; just different. And as if in answer to a call which had certainly never been uttered except, perhaps, in his mind, Phil was suddenly there in the room, bringing him a clean pair of slacks and a shirt from the airing cupboard.

"Good morning, mudlark! How do you feel this morning?"

He felt strange; larger than usual, more responsible, and more subdued. Big with all the things he had to think about. But beyond all question, he felt good. Good, in a state of well-being; and good, virtuous.

"I feel fine. Is it really that time? And I've got to go to the police station, haven't I?" He sat up, solemn-faced, remembering.

"Mummy!" The sudden charged softness of his voice warned her what was coming, but he was longer about framing it than she had expected, and the end-product, when it emerged, was a revelation.

"Mummy, *who was I*?"

Her heart gave a leap of joy and triumph. She thought: Poor Simon! She laid Paddy's clean clothes on a chair, and came and sat down on the edge of his bed. Flushed and bemused from long sleep, he faced her earnestly and trustingly, and waited for an answer. It mattered, just to the private thinking he had to do about himself; but it couldn't affect what they had between them now.

"You know," he said, "what I mean."

"Yes, I know. Your mother was a very nice girl, a good friend of ours, Paddy. She was only twenty-one when she died, from some illness that came on after you were born. And her husband—your father—You know him, Paddy. You know him very well, and he's very fond of you. You know him as Uncle Simon."

He didn't exclaim, his face didn't show surprise, or consternation, or relief, or pleasure, or anything else but the same charged gravity. He accepted it, and sat digesting it.

"His wife died," said Phil, "and left you on his hands.

He was just beginning to be well-known then, and he had a contract for his first big tour. He couldn't take a baby with him. And I'd lost one only a few months before, and the doctors said I couldn't have another. So you mustn't blame him too much. He loved his wife very much, and he was wretched about losing her, and wanted to get away. It wasn't just fear of losing his big opportunity."

Since she had invited this single combat, she felt obliged to conduct it scrupulously; and besides, one should never allow a child to contemplate the possibility that he may have failed to make himself loved. But was this a child facing her? The fluffy crest and slender neck and un-formed forehead said yes; the grave eyes and something in the set of the face suggested that this juvenile image was already a little out of date.

"It doesn't mean he didn't love you," said Phil firmly. But he didn't, she thought honestly; he wasn't a person to whom babies were quite human beings at all, and he isn't alone in that, it's something he couldn't help. "Well, you've got to know him pretty well, this visit. He hasn't shown any want of affection, has he?"

Paddy received the revelation in silence, and continued to ponder with an almost forbidding concentration.

"O.K., Mummy, I see. Thanks for telling me. Now we're all straight." He slid his legs out of bed. "I'd better get a move on, or Mr. Hewitt will be sending an escort for me. But I don't know that I'm going to be much use to him, am I? I mean, my little trek isn't going to tell him who knocked old Trethuan on the head and tossed him in the sea, is it?"

"That reminds me," said Phil, glad of the distraction. "Do you know what I found in your pocket last night?" She brought the little gold coin, and displayed it trium-phantly in her palm.

"Oh, that!" he said, rather disappointingly. And then, as his eyes took in the design and the colour of it, which seemed to be totally unfamiliar: "Gosh, is *that* what it turned out to be? But it looks really something." He took it and turned it about curiously, examining it with astonished delight. "What is it? Do you know?"

"You're a fine one!" said Phil, amused. "First you say: 'Oh, that!' Then you start goggling at it as if you'd never seen it before."

"But, silly," he said, laughing, "I never have seen it before. It was pitch dark in there, I told you, that's why I had to give up and turn back in the end. I've *felt* it before, though."

"You found it in this passage in the cave?"

"Yes, way along it as far as I went. I fell over a bit of rock and went down on my hands, and this thing was sticking in my palm. Well, I could tell it was a coin, but all I thought was, somebody else exploring must have had a hole in his pocket, and I was a shilling up. It looks like *gold*," said Paddy disbelievingly. "Could it be?"

"I think it could, you know. Guineas and half-guineas were minted in gold, and this seems to be a Queen Anne guinea. You could show it to somebody at the museum, to make sure."

"You mean it's really worth a guinea?" His eyes were wide with visions of wealth, and had lost for a moment their look of solemn preoccupation.

"More, I should imagine, if it's genuine, and I can't think of a reason why it shouldn't be. But it might be treasure trove, technically, we should have to find out about that."

"I thought there'd be a catch in it." He grinned at her cheerfully enough, still having at least the thrill of discovery. "But there might be more of them, did you think of that? Smugglers might have hidden them somewhere there." She could feel him suddenly planning, and checking, and contemplating a barrier he might have to get round before he could proceed. Moments of crisis boil up so abruptly out of nowhere. "Mummy!"

The careful, gentle, tentative voice nerved itself, moving in on her. Here it comes, Phil, she thought, and whatever you do there mustn't be any hesitation.

"Mummy, you don't mind if I go back there and take another look? With a torch, of course, this time."

It was a stiff fence for both of them. Knowing he'd frightened her half to death once, and she'd hardly had time yet to get over it, terrified of being babied, but aware that it might be hard for her to give him his head to frighten her in the same way again, he couldn't quite manage the right easy tone. But that was something she mustn't let him realise she had noticed.

"No, of course I don't mind, darling. Take Daddy's big torch, there's a new battery in it. Don't want to risk getting left in the dark again. Do I get a commission, if the hoard turns out to be legally yours?"

After a brief, blank instant of astonished relief and admiration, shaken to the heart at finding himself trusted without even a caution, he said gruffly: "You bet you do! We'll go halves."

"Low tide's about a quarter to twelve. You'll be able to get in any time after ten. So hurry and get up to Mr. Hewitt, and then you'll have time enough before lunch." Blessed reassurance, he wouldn't risk missing his lunch, not on a day when he was happy, not for all the guineas Queen Anne ever minted.

"I'll be careful," he volunteered even more gruffly, and dug his toes hastily into his slippers and headed for the door.

There he checked, ears suddenly pricked, catching the unmistakable sound of Simon's Porsche starting up in the yard. Phil saw him stiffen, and the resolute shade of thought came down again upon his face. There was a relationship still to be adjusted somehow, and it wasn't going to be easy.

She wished she could guess what was going on in his mind, but the set of his face told her nothing. All that charm and glamour and excitement suddenly his for the claiming, and more than ready to fall into his lap— if only he would say something to give her a clue! But when he did make his one pregnant comment, it wasn't much help to her.

"I suppose I'm more fun now," said Paddy bafflingly, and whisked away to the bathroom.

::   ::

"I'm sorry," he was saying, three-quarters of an hour later, in Hewitt's office overlooking the square, "I don't seem to have been much help. But I really didn't look up at the Dragon's Head at all, and I didn't see a soul until Dominic came yelling at me. It isn't as if I'd seen anyone fall from up there, you see. I don't even know anything accurate about times, because I ran down in my trunks, like I always do, and I didn't have my watch. I'm sorry!"

"Well, there it is," agreed Hewitt, no more nor less lugubrious than usual, but distinctly more loquacious, solid and fresh behind his shabby desk, with George Felse and Simon Towne in silent attendance, one on either side. "Can't be helped, laddie. Don't you worry about it any more."

"And you don't think my passage in the cave, and that guinea—if it really is a guinea?—you don't think they're anything to do with Treverra?"

"I didn't say that, Paddy, my boy. I think it's unlikely, but I didn't say I wasn't interested. But I've no time to investigate that to-day."

"Well, is it all right if I go and explore there again myself? I haven't got much time left, you see, I go back to school Monday." School was the boarding-house of the best local grammar school, twelve miles inland. Its shadow cast a light cloud over the last week of his holidays, but promised escape, at least, from his present difficulties. He hadn't once seemed to look at Simon since he balked in the office doorway on finding him there, but he hadn't missed a single shade of expression that crossed the somewhat drawn and sombre face. He saw it tighten now, saw the quick flash of uneasy brown eyes in George's direction.

"My mother's given me permission," said Paddy, with immense dignity.

"I've no objection, laddie," said Hewitt heartily. "You go ahead, and good luck. Let me know if you find out where the treasure's buried." He saw Paddy's eloquent eyes rest calculatingly upon the small gold coin that lay before him on the desk, and palmed and tossed it to him so smoothly that the act seemed spontaneous. "Here, better keep your sample by you. You'll let me see it again if necessary, I'm sure."

Paddy's smile blazed like the sun. The little glitter of metal vanished into his ready palm and into his pocket. "Yes, of *course*!"

"Why don't you show the place to Dominic?" suggested Simon, lightly and quickly. "You just about owe him that."

And Mr. Felse, equally easily: "He'd certainly be glad to come with you. I look like being busy for a while, and he won't want to go souvenir-shopping with his mother, that's sure. Give him a ring, Paddy."

"I will," said Paddy politely. "Thank you."

He was pretty quick on the draw, was Mr. Felse, but of course a detective-inspector would have to be. He got Uncle Simon's message as fast as I did, thought Paddy, withdrawing aloofly from the room. He didn't want me to go back in the cave alone. Mummy still trusts me, but he doesn't. He's afraid something may happen to me.

And in the instant he saw it in reverse, and was dazzled. Uncle Simon, who can do everything better than anyone else, who goes everywhere, and ventures everything, and doesn't know what it is to be afraid for himself, he's afraid for *me*. He *does* care about me. Uncle Simon that was. Now I don't know what to call him. I don't know what he is.

I know what I am, though. I know *who* I am. And Mummy cares about me, too, and maybe she was just as afraid—more, because she's a woman. But all the same, she trusted me, and didn't even say: Take Dominic with you.

Meantime, it was hardly Dominic's fault, and you could see their point of view, and all that. So he'd do just what he'd said he'd do, and call him and invite him to come along. He was a little bit prefect-type, to be honest, but it was difficult not to be at that age; and he'd been jolly decent last night, and had the tact to vanish into the background as soon as the fussing began. He deserved to be rescued from souvenir-shopping.

      : :   : :

"Well, that didn't get us much forrarder," observed Hewitt, when the door had closed and Paddy's feet were clattering down the stairs. "No surprise, really, I didn't think it would. So here we still are with two bodies that shouldn't have been there, and—don't forget this little detail—minus one that should.

"With the older body we still haven't got much to go on. The first job is to identify him. According to the reports so far he was about thirty years old, about six feet tall, and a pretty husky specimen. His ears were pierced, and there's a thin gold ring still in one of 'em. The body shows no injuries except to the skull, and those were clearly the cause of death. It looks as if he was bashed on the head from behind, maybe two or three blows, with a solid and probably jagged object, such as a lump of rock. The fragments of cloth suggest he was a seaman, most likely a fisherman."

"Which means probably a local man," said Simon intently.

"It doesn't necessarily follow, but everything rather indicates it as a probability. He's been dead between two and three years—certainly not two centuries. The one really good lead for identifying him is in his jaws. He's got a lot of very good dental work, most likely all done in one series of treatments after a long period of neglect. Whoever did that job on him will have it on record, and he'll know his own work again. It means we've got to get on to every dentist here and maybe up and down the coast, but it's only a matter of time, and we'll find him. And then, with any luck, we'll know who we've got down there.

"Now the other one, he's a very different matter. Here we have a fellow everyone knows, who was seen alive as late as four o'clock last Wednesday, and according to the medical evidence and the set of the tides must have been dead before ten o'clock the same night. The blow or blows that left that mark on his face didn't do more than knock him out, which seems to have been the object. He's otherwise more or less undamaged. He drowned in salt water, and was then put in the Treverra vault. And though Miss Rachel's key was in your possession during the material time, Mr. Towne, we now know that another key exists, and was kept in a place where anyone who had a little inside knowledge or a bit of luck could get at it. That leaves us a pretty wide field. It may have occurred to you, as a limiting factor, that surely only somebody who didn't know the vault was about to be opened could think of it as a good hiding-place for a murdered man. But even if we accept that—and I wouldn't put too much reliance on its importance—the field's still wide enough.

"Now here we've got an unfriendly man who kept himself very much to himself, and usually managed to grate on other people so much that they were glad to let him. Obviously we're obliged to make a pretty thorough check on the movements of his son-in-law, because it's no secret that young Jim had a good many breezes with Trethuan before he got Rose away from him, and relations have been strained, to say the least of it, ever since. I'm not saying I think Jim Pollard makes a very likely murderer, but he's got a temper, and these things happen without much warning sometimes. There are holes in Jim's alibi that won't be easy to fill. He was down to the yard at the south end of Maymouth, Wednesday afternoon, for some timber for a little repair job at home, and then he did one or two more errands for paint and stuff round the town, and ended up working late on an old boat he's got beached in Pentarno haven, so he says. Which makes him mobile and at large but for the times of his various calls, and leaves plenty of time between for an unexpected brush with Rose's dad, supposing he met him in a nasty mood.

"However, he's just one possibility among many. If I should ask you, now, what's the oddest thing about Trethuan's own behaviour in the last days of his life, what would you say?"

He had looked at Simon, but Simon held his tongue. When the guileless stare turned upon George he responded promptly: "Why was he so insistent that the vault must not be opened?"

"Exactly! Why? Religious objections? Superstition? That would account for anyone in his position criticising and prophesying evil, yes. But by all accounts this was more than that. He was desperate about it. Is that too strong, Mr. Towne?"

"No," said Simon shortly, "that's how he struck me."

"So what was it that made it so urgent? Now I hear most of what goes on around here, and I don't mind telling you openly, I know all about your sporting warning issued in the Dragon bar on Wednesday night, Mr. Towne. And I saw—and so did Mr. Felse, if you didn't—the signs that the vault had been artistically swept and garnished and sanded over again before I got to it, and presumably before you did, on Friday. It's an old and time-honoured profession, is smuggling. You know it still goes on, I know it still goes on. I doubt if there's a licensee along this coast who doesn't get a drop of the real stuff that way. We know the vault was used as a liquor store, we know there was a nice, handy key, the one Sam Shubrough came by as an innocent child. And we know they won't use the same place again, if it's any reassurance to you—not since they cleared out their contraband, whenever they did. There wasn't any sense of desperation there. *They* didn't care a toot when you tipped 'em the wink, they just took the tip, and shifted their store to a safer place. And slipped you one on the house as an acknowledgment, I shouldn't wonder. Only one person was really concerned, and that was Trethuan. A lone wolf who wouldn't be wanted in any such confraternity, and who wouldn't want to be in it, anyhow.

"So I'm telling you, I don't believe smuggling or contraband had anything whatever to do with Trethuan's death, and I don't think you need worry about any of the otherwise law-abiding chaps around here who don't feel it any sin to slip a few kegs of brandy past the preventives.

They're not my job. Murder is. And we're left with Trethuan and the something that made it absolutely vital to him that Treverra should rest in peace. Always supposing he'd been resting there at all, which as it turned out he wasn't. Did Zeb have something private and dangerous of his own that came over with the brandy? I doubt it. No, more likely his preoccupation was about something quite separate from theirs. There's only one certain thing we know about it. It was somewhere in the vault. Why else should he be so desperate to stop you from opening it?"

"And why couldn't he move it," said George, "since apparently he could put it there in the first place?"

"*And where is it?*" added Simon. "The place is as bare as the palm of your hand but for those two stone coffins. One of those we've exhausted already. There's nowhere left but Mrs. Treverra's coffin."

"And that's exactly it, Mr. Towne. You represent Miss Rachel's interest in this matter. I'm going to suggest to you that we ought to open the second coffin, too. The Vicar thinks he can justifiably sanction it, on the strength of the permission already given for her husband. If you're prepared to join me and come along down to St. Nectan's right now, we can at least see if there's anything there to account for Zeb Trethuan's acting like a desperate man."

"For the record," said Simon, his eyes kindling golden-brown with curiosity, "maybe we should. If it turns out to be full of Swiss watches that have never paid duty, then we shall be getting somewhere."

"According to precedent to date," said George dryly and ruefully, as they went down the stairs, "the one thing that certainly won't be in it is Mrs. Treverra!"

::   ::

But that was where George was wrong. For when they had carefully lowered Jan Treverra's coffin-lid with slings to the floor of the vault, and prised the smaller stone lid beneath it, with its fine, defiant flourish of cryptic verse, out of its seating, when they had levered it clear and lowered it to rest beside its fellow, when they stood staring into the coffin, it was plain to be seen that the lady was all too surely there.

The shadow slid from over her almost reluctantly. A gush of fine dust ascended into the beam of their lanterns, and a dry, dead, nostalgic scent, as though pressed flowers, long since paper-fine and drained of nature, had disintegrated into powder at a touch. The outer air spilled in upon her, flowing over the broken and displaced lid of the wooden coffin that had once held her, and the frozen turbulence of silks and woollen cloth that overflowed from the box, stirred by the displacement of air, billowed for one instant buoyant and stable in their sight, and then collapsed together with a faint, whispering sigh, crumbling away at hems and folds into fragmentary rags.

A subsiding drift of dust and tindery cloth settled and fluttered down into the grave, disclosing the small, convulsed bones of hands and arms and drawn-up knees that thrust vainly and frenziedly upward, a shapely skull arched back in anguished effort among a nest of crumbling silks and laces, and the withered black of once-luxuriant hair, powdered over with the drab of perished silk and the fine, incorruptible dust of death.

Morwenna did not rest in peace. Contorted, struggling, fighting to force her way out, she seemed for a moment to be about to rise and reach her fragile, skeleton hands to them. Then even her bones began to rustle and crumble stealthily, settling lower and lower before their eyes into the stone tomb in which she had quite certainly been buried alive.

CHAPTER VII

SATURDAY NOON

"Oh, it's you at last, miss, is it?" said Miss Rachel into
the telephone, in her most belligerent tones, for fear she
should be suspected of even the least shade of penitence.
"And about time, too! What do you think you are doing,
absenting yourself in this undisciplined way, and where,
may I ask, are you doing it?"

"I'm at the Dragon. You told me not to bother to come
back, remember? But as a matter of fact, I did 'phone
Alice, pretty late, after we found Paddy. I beg his pardon,
after he came back, I should have said. He wasn't lost,
he knew only too well where he was. And all your fault,
in case nobody else has raised enough courage to tell you.
Me? What have I got to lose? You as good as fired me."

"I did nothing of the sort! But if you're not back here
pretty quickly, miss, I will! You can't leave without giving
me a month's notice, and even if you did, I wouldn't take
it, so don't be so uppish. Is Paddy there? I thought I
heard his voice a minute ago."

"Yes, he's here." He was giggling like a girl in the
background, but a little conscience-stricken, too. "He
came up to ask Dominic to go out somewhere with him, and
if you want to know, I'm going, too. I like handsome young
escorts, and now I've got two of 'em. Don't expect me
back before lunch, and I'll be late for that. What? No,
don't be silly. We were just rather late, and I was very
dirty and hungry, so I accepted Mrs. Felse's offer to come
here with them for dinner and borrow some clothes from
her. Then I called Alice, and she said you knew Paddy
was O.K., and you were just about exhausted with worry
and then relief, and had gone to bed. So I thought I
might as well stay here overnight, as Bunty was kind

enough to lend me everything I needed. O.K., so you weren't worried. Then why were you carrying on like a broody hen? Well, tell Alice you weren't, she told me. Half-way up the wall, she said—Yes, sure you were right, cleared the air like a thunderstorm. All right, I'll be home this afternoon. Yes, he's all right. Do you want a word with him?"

Paddy smoothed her in one breathless sentence : " Hallo, Aunt Rachel, I'm terribly sorry about the rest of the apricots, it was all a mix-up, I meant to come back. Would some of them be all right to-morrow? Mummy's making jam with those. No, I don't mind, really I don't. I'm glad. Yes, I do mean it. Can we keep Tamsin for to-day? She was the one who found me last night—one of the two, that is, Dominic was the other. 'Ess, me dear, I'll be up-along soon as I can. To-morrow for sure, because I'm going back to school Monday, you know. O.K., I'll tell her. 'Bye, Aunt Rachel!"

He hung up, grinning. " She says to tell you Alice has instructions not to keep lunch hot for you."

"Good!" said Tamsin, linking her other arm in Dominic's. " That means I've got the whole day off. Come on, let's go and pan gold in Paddy's cave."

They went down the steep path from the Dragon, where Simon had risked his neck on Paddy's cycle, three abreast, linked and light-hearted. At the edge of the harbour they halted to buy three immense cones of candy-floss, and went down the harbour steps in single file, flourishing them like torch-bearers in a procession, and nibbling the fringes like fire-eaters. They paid no attention to anyone or anything but their own mid-September holiday happiness, reprieved from yesterday's shadow. But a girl who was just hurrying out of the narrow, rocky alley behind the six colour-washed cottages of Cliffside Row checked and drew back at sight of them, and stood in the shadow of the rocks, watching them recede, linked and hilarious, down the slate-coloured sands.

The tide was nearing its lowest ebb, and beyond the pebbly stretches the finer sand gleamed moist and bright in a watery sun. The three young people, the taller boy, the visitor, on the right, young Paddy Rossall on the left, Tamsin Holt in the middle with her arm about Paddy's shoulders and the other boy's arm about hers, bore steadily sidelong into the cliff face, and halted to finish their hectic pink torches before they vanished into the black mouth of the Dragon's Hole.

Paddy looked back up the beach towards the coloured cardboard stage set, the impossibly charming and gay toy theatre of the harbour and the town. He saw another flare of candy-floss, primrose-gold, burning at the corner of the dark alley behind the cottages, and recognised Rose Pollard, a round, soft, appealing doll in neutral Shetland sweater and tartan trews, standing there braced and alert. She seemed—he couldn't be sure, but that was how it struck him—she seemed to be watching them, and wondering, and hesitating. And when she moved at last, it was to draw back softly into the shadow; but his eyes, following movement rather than colours, assured him that she had not gone away, and his intuition, already sharpened beyond ordinary this morning, warned him that she had not stopped watching.

::   ::

"I can't believe it," said Tamsin disgustedly. "We've walked how far?—more than half a mile underground, and suddenly the whole thing folds up in a blank wall. And you said yourself the stone's been worked with tools in places, so somebody was interested in improving the passage for use. Why would it just stop, without arriving anywhere?"

Dominic's eyes followed the beam of Paddy's torch from stone ceiling to stone floor. To call it a blank wall that faced them was simplifying things; it was a rough confusion of broken planes, sealing off the small chamber into which the passage had opened. But quite certainly there was no cleft nor hole in it through which they could pass. This was the end of the journey.

"Maybe the passage was an end in itself," he said. "There's room among some of these side-pockets we've passed to store any amount of contraband. The whole complex could be a pretty good hiding-place. And they may have taken steps to hide the entrance even better, when it was in use."

"But, look," said Paddy acutely, "if the passage was to be the cache, they didn't need half a mile of it, a hundred yards would have done. They could have got a ship-load of stuff in that first bulge. You don't chip your way along half a mile underground unless you're aiming to *get* somewhere."

"I have to admit," agreed Tamsin thoughtfully, after pondering this for a minute, "that he's got something there."

"Do you suppose we've missed a turning somewhere? It may go on in another direction."

"We could have a more thorough look on the way back. We've got time, it's not much after twelve. And there's nothing for us here."

They turned back rather reluctantly, all the same; nobody likes going back by the same route. It is, as Paddy had rightly observed, a fundamental predilection of human nature to want to get somewhere, even if most arrivals turn out to be disappointing.

The floor on which they walked had been smoothed in places by stones deliberately laid. Sometimes it was naked rock, sometimes this levelled causeway, and sometimes, especially where the narrow cleft opened out into a broader passage, there was deep, fine grey sand. With a light, the whole half-mile of it was easy, no more than a stony walk; and all these later reaches were dry, for over the entire length the level climbed very gently, and bore away inland from the Dragon's Hole at a brisk right incline.

"Where do you suppose we are?" asked Paddy as they turned back, playing his light ahead of them on both rough walls. "Half a mile is farther than the neck, we must be right under the high part of the town."

"I don't think we've borne as far to the right as that," objected Dominic. "I'd say somewhere just the other side the Head, under the dunes."

"It's so straightforward here," said Tamsin, stepping out merrily in the lead, "you hardly need a light." And promptly on the word she tripped over a stone that tilted treacherously out of the sandy floor, and went down with a squeak of protest on hands and knees.

Dominic and Paddy both reached solicitous hands to help her up, but for a moment she sat scowling, dusting her hands and examining her nylons. "Damn! Somebody owes me a new pair of stockings." A ladder was trickling playfully downward from her right knee.

"I'll buy you some new ones with my guinea," offered Paddy generously. "That was pretty much how I found it, actually, only I had more excuse, because I didn't have a light that time. You sure you're not sitting on a pirate's hoard?"

"Not unless he hoarded granite sand. But there was something sharp, look, it broke the skin." She sifted fine sand through her fingers, probed the indentation her knee had made, and raised from beneath the surface a thin ring of yellow wire, with edges that barely met. "That's the secret weapon. Not a pirate's hoard, but maybe a smuggler's ear-ring." She rubbed it on her sleeve, and it gleamed encouragingly. "I believe that's what it is. It looks like gold wire."

They ran the torch carefully over every corner of the sanded floor, but found nothing more. Tamsin pocketed her find, and they resumed their methodical walk back. There were broken bays in the rocks here and there to be explored, but all of them proved to be dead ends; and as they drew nearer to the Dragon's Hole tiny trickles of water filtered down from the walls and channelled the sand of the floor.

They reached the seaward end of the tunnel, where the low, screened entrance hole shrank to thigh-height, and doubled upon itself midway in an optical illusion of solid rock. They crawled through on hands and knees, and stood upright again in the upper reaches of the Dragon's Hole. When they had dropped down the slopes of shale and shell to where the light of the September day penetrated, there were still a few children playing on the sand, but even these were being called away to lunch by parents and elder sisters. The midday quiet was descending on Maymouth's beaches. Far down the glistening shore the tide had turned, and was beginning to lip its way back towards the town, but it would be two hours yet before it covered the cavern again.

"You could come and have lunch with us," said Dominic, "if you'd like to. Tamsin's staying. We could ring up your mother and tell her." But he made the offer rather hesitantly, and was not surprised when it was politely refused. Paddy hadn't seen his mother for all of three hours, and there are times when three hours is a long time. Moreover, he had to demonstrate, rather than claim, that he was a responsible person who paid attention to the times of high and low tide, and could be trusted not to take any more chances.

"Thanks awfully, but I think I ought to go home."

"Well, come and have an ice with us, anyhow."

Paddy jumped at this offer. They climbed the steep path from the harbour to the Dragon's Head, and turned in by the first pale cliff-track towards the Dragon Hotel.

"Better put this with your guinea," said Tamsin, extracting the thin gold ring from her pocket. "I don't suppose it's anything much, but hang on to it, and time will show."

"Do you think we should tell Mr. Hewitt about it? I told him I was coming to have another look at the passage, but he wasn't much interested."

"Question of priorities," said Dominic with courteous gravity. "Tell him about it, but leave it till he's got time for it. He's probably got a dozen lines to follow up, and some of 'em more urgent than this. He'll work his way round to it."

They were walking close to the grassy edge of the cliff, where it overhung the beach and the harbour. Paddy looked down, from the painted operetta-set of Cliffside Row to the mouth of the blow-hole. The children were all gone now, the whole sickle of moist shore was empty. Only one lance of movement caught his eye.

From the narrow alley behind the cottages darted the figure of a girl, hugging the shadow of the cliff. She had tied a dark chiffon scarf over her candy-floss torch of pale hair, but Paddy knew her all the same, by her fawn-coloured sweater and Black-Watch-tartan legs. She ran head-down, hugging something small and shapeless under her arm. Because of the overhang he lost sight of her for a full minute, then she reappeared close to the deep shadow of the Dragon's Hole, and darted into it, and vanished.

He opened his mouth to call the attention of his companions to her, and then after all he held his tongue, and walked on with them in silence. But he couldn't get Rose Pollard out of his mind. And the more he thought of her, the clearer did it seem to him that she had been in the act of launching herself on this same errand earlier this morning, and then had drawn back when she saw them go down the beach ahead of her, and enter the cave. She had watched them every step of the way, he recalled now the stillness and tension of that small figure standing at the edge of the sunlight. The tide had dropped just clear of the entrance then, the beach had been otherwise almost deserted, only they had prevented whatever it was Rose wanted to do. Almost certainly she had watched them emerge again into sunlight and walk back to the harbour steps and the cliff path. Then, with the last of the playing children called home to lunch, she had found the coast clear at last.

For what? He had known her since he was a small boy, she had acted as baby-sitter several times for his mother, and he had liked her because she was kind and pretty and soft, and he could twist her round his finger, stay up as long as he liked, make all the mess he wanted in his bath, and ignore the finer points of washing. She wouldn't have the resolution to do anything dangerous or underhanded, and she wouldn't have the wits to cover it up for long even if she tried it. Unless, perhaps, for Jim she could rise to things she wouldn't dare attempt for herself? It was her father who was dead, and she hadn't liked her father any better than anyone else had, and Jim had detested him, because of her. But they couldn't have done anything bad, he wouldn't believe it. They were both too open, not for darkness and secrecy. Not for caves! Rose was frightened of the dark. What *was* she doing there?

Mute and abstracted, he ate his way through a cassata, and made his farewells. But once he was out of sight of the hotel terrace and back on the cliff path, it was towards Maymouth that he turned. He slid recklessly down the whitening, late-summer grass to the harbour, clattered down the steps, and homed like a racing pigeon into the gaping mouth of the Dragon's Hole.

::   ::

She wasn't in the open part of the cave, he knew that intuitively as soon as he crept into the dark interior. There were no echoes, only the very faint and ubiquitous murmur of water, that was inaudible when there were voices and movements to drown it. She might have gone right through into the haven at Pentarno, which would still be dry at this hour; but he scrambled purposefully straight through until the daylight met him again, and the great waste of the beach and the dunes lay within sight, and there was no Rose to be seen crossing the sands.

In his heart he'd known all along where she must be. He abandoned the stony channel, and climbed inland, as quietly as he could, until he stood hesitating unhappily over the entrance to the tunnel.

He couldn't follow her in there without meeting her face to face, and somehow he couldn't bring himself to precipitate a situation like that, at least not until he knew what he was doing. He looked round him for the best cover, compressed his slight person into a screened corner as close as he dared to the passage, and sat there silently, his arms wound round his knees, his heart thumping. She couldn't possibly stay long, whatever she had to do there, because she had to return by the same way, and to make good her retreat from the cave before the tide engulfed it. But if she didn't come, what must he do? Get out in time himself, and tell Jim? But Jim must surely know already. Husbands and wives were in each other's confidence, weren't they? Tell Hewitt, then? Or ought he to stay there and take care of Rose? But he *couldn't* do that to his mother, not again! He was getting hopelessly confused as to where his duty lay.

Rose spared him a decision. Before he heard her footsteps he saw a thin, pale pencil of light filter out of the rock wall, and waver across the shaly floor. She was hurrying, perhaps afraid of the tide, though she had still plenty of time by his reckoning. He heard the pebbles rasping, and uneven, running steps suddenly ending in a soft thud, as she threw herself down to creep through the low opening. The light of her torch leaped and fluttered with every thrust of the hand that held it. She clawed her way through, careless of the noise she made, as though a demon had been hard at her heels. When she scrambled to her feet, he saw the flickering light cast from below upon her pale hair, from which the scarf had been dragged back on to her shoulders. He saw her face twisted hopelessly into a child's mask of anguish, smeared with tears, the soft mouth contorted, the round chin jerking.

She blundered away from him down the slope, slipping and recovering in her frantic haste, and he heard the convulsed sobbing of her breath, and a faint, horrified whimpering that made the short hairs rise in the nape of his neck. The rattle of pebbles from under her feet receded and was still.

He sat for some minutes hugging his knees and shaking, reluctant to creep out after her where he must be seen. It didn't seem decent to let her guess that he'd been spying upon her in that condition. It didn't seem decent now that he had ever thought of doing it, but he had, and he hadn't meant any harm to her, rather the opposite. Better not to say anything to anybody, because whatever she was so frightened and so unhappy about, Rose couldn't have done any wrong, she had no wrong in her, she was too soft and mild. Better to go through the Hole to the Pentarno side; he might have to roll up his slacks and wade out at the entrance that side, because it lay a couple of feet or so lower than the Maymouth end. But it wouldn't be any worse than that, and he could still be home before his mother began to get worried.

He scurried down the slope to the thread of water that was gathering in the channel, and clambered hastily through the Hole again, to splash through the first encroaching foam and take to his heels up the Pentarno beach. The remembered vision of Rose Pollard hung before his eyes every step of the way, both arms spread for balance, the glow of the torch flailing in her right hand.

One thing at least was certain. When she came back from her mysterious errand, she had no longer been carrying anything under her arm.

CHAPTER VIII

SATURDAY EVENING

PHIL WAS WASHING UP after tea when Hewitt called. She put her head in at the door of the living-room to report: "For you, Simon. Mr. Hewitt says the pathologist's come to have a look at Mrs. Treverra's body, and if you and Tim would care to be present, he'd be grateful. I suppose he wants to have the family represented, so that there can't be any complaints or anything later. Shall I tell him you'll be along?"

All three of them had looked up sharply at the message, Paddy sensitive to the quiver of feeling on the air, and stirred out of his unnaturally subdued quietness. All afternoon Tim and Phil had been exchanging anxious glances over his head, and wondering how long to let him alone, how soon to shake him out of his abstraction. A very dutiful, mute, well-behaved boy who sat and thought was not at all what they were used to.

"How about it, Tim? I don't say it's the pleasantest

thing in the world to see, but if we can learn anything from it, I think we should."

"I'll come, I want to. It's a hell of a thing," said Tim soberly.

"Then he says in a quarter of an hour, at St. Nectan's. They don't propose to disturb her, not unless there's absolute need. I'll tell him you'll be there."

Tim looked at Paddy. There was no guessing what was in his head, but it could only be the shocks and readjustments of yesterday that were still preoccupying him. Unless directly addressed, he hadn't once said a word to Simon, and they had refrained from discussing the inexplicable tragedy of Morwenna in front of him. But sooner or later he had to learn to move and breathe in the same air with Simon again, and find some sort of terms on which he could live with him, and he might just as well begin at once.

"How about you, Paddy?" invited Tim after a moment's hesitation. "Come along with us for the ride?"

The serious face brightened, wavered and smiled. "I bet that means I don't get to come in," he said, but he got up from his chair with every appearance of pleasure.

"I think I'd rather you didn't. But I'll tell you about it as we go."

"O.K., Dad, I'll come, anyhow." He hadn't been with Tim very much during the day, and he found that he wanted to. To sit by him in the front seat of the Mini, and touch shoulders with him now and again, was comfort, pleasure and reassurance. Subdued and amenable, he wasn't going to ask any favours; if he was required to sit in the car while they went down into the vault, he'd do it, and not even creep to the top of the steps to peer down in the hope of a glimpse of forbidden sights. It was his pleasure to please Tim. You can be demonstrative with mothers, but showing fathers how you feel about them is not quite so simple, you use what offers, and hope they'll get the idea.

They threaded the sunken lane, halted at the coast road, and crossed it to the track among the dunes. The smell of the evening was the smell of the autumnal sea and the fading grasses.

"I didn't know they were thinking of opening Mrs. Treverra's coffin, too. Why did they? Was that this morning?"

Any other time he would have been asking Simon, hanging over the back of the seat and feeding on his looks and words like a puppy begging for cake. Now he sat close and asked Tim, in his quiet, young baritone, touchingly grave and tentative.

"Yes, this morning. After you left, I suppose it must have been. I wasn't there. Mr. Hewitt thought it necessary to search every possible place in the vault, because it seems there must have been something there to account for Trethuan's not wanting it opened. And the only place that hadn't been searched already was Morwenna's coffin. So they opened that, too." Tim eased the Mini down into the rutted, drifting sand, and was silent for a moment. "She's there, Paddy. It isn't like the other one, she is there. Well, this chap's going to tell us whether the body that's there is from the right time, and so on, but I don't think there's much doubt. But what's terribly wrong is that she —well, she isn't at peace. She's fully dressed—she *was*— and she was trying to get out. She—must have been alive when they left her there. It could happen. Sometimes it has happened."

He had felt the young, solid shoulder stiffen in unbelieving horror, and he wanted to soften the picture, to set it two centuries away, like a dream or a sad song.

"They hadn't modern methods or modern knowledge. There could be conditions like death. They weren't to blame. And thank God, they couldn't have known. Only we know, when it's all over, two hundred years and more. Like 'The Mistletoe Bough.' It wouldn't be quite like you think. The air would give out on her, you see. She'd only have what was inside the stone coffin, and then, gradually, sleep. It wouldn't be long."

Simon might not have been there. There was no one

else in the car. Paddy leaned closer by an inch, delicately and gratefully.

"It could look like a struggle, but be only very brief. Very soon she grew drowsy. Only she stayed like that, you see, fighting to lift the lid and get out. She slept like that. And when she was dead—Well, you've read her epitaph. This makes me think she wrote it herself. I don't even know why, but it does."

Paddy said, in a small but still adult voice, perhaps even a note or two nearer the bass register than usual: "I always thought she was so beautiful."

"So did I. She'll find him again, you can bet on that. She wasn't the sort to let death stop her."

The Mini turned in to the left among the dunes. The little open lantern of St. Nectan's stood clear against the sky.

"It wasn't ugly," said Simon unexpectedly from the back seat. "A scent, and a puff of air, and a little dust. She was very little, like in her picture, and all muffled up in a travelling cloak with a hood—at least, I think so. She had masses of black hair, and such tiny bones."

Paddy said nothing more. He sat almost oblivious when they got out of the car and left him there between the shadowy dunes. He woke out of his daze when he heard the strange voices, and turned his head to see them met and greeted by Hewitt, with George Felse in attendance, and a stranger who must be the police pathologist. He watched them unlock the padlock on the gate, and go in single file down the steep staircase. He heard the heavy door below swing wide, but he didn't move. If the window of the car had not been open, he would not have heard the raised tones of their voices, like gasps of amazement and consternation rising hollowly out of the grave.

Something was wrong, down there. Something was not as they had expected it to be. Paddy put out a hand to open the door of the car, and then drew it back, shivering, afraid to want to know.

But you can't turn your back on knowledge, just because it may be uncomfortable. Supposing someone else should need what you know? Someone who belongs to you, and doesn't know how much you know already?

He slipped out of the car, and crept close to the rail of the vault. The open doorway showed him nothing but a corner of Treverra's empty tomb, and half of George Felse and all of Tim, hiding from him even the foot of the second coffin. But the voices sailed up to him clearly, roused and brittle, and in signal agreement.

"None of it was there this morning," said Hewitt. "There was *nothing* with her in the coffin. All of us but Mr. Rossall were here, we know what we uncovered."

"We couldn't possibly have missed seeing this," said Simon. "Even if we didn't disturb or touch her, we looked pretty carefully. It's enough to make you look carefully, isn't it? Well, she'd none of all this with her then. Nothing!"

"But if you've had both keys in your own hands all the time, and you locked up again carefully this morning," said the one strange voice with dry mildness, "it would seem to be impossible."

"It is, damned impossible, but it's happened." It was the first time Paddy had ever heard Hewitt sound exasperated. "Take a look at this, this is real enough, isn't it? That wasn't here, none of this was here spilled round her feet, at eleven o'clock this morning. But it's here now at six in the evening. And I'm telling you—I'm telling myself, for that matter—this place has been locked all that time, and I've had both keys on me. And tell me, just tell me, why should anyone, guilty or innocent or crazy or what, bring *this* here and leave it for us to find?"

He plunged a hand suddenly into something that rattled and rang like the loose change in a careless woman's handbag, and brandished across the coffin, for one moment full into Paddy's line of vision, a handful of coins and small trinkets that gleamed, in spite of all the discolorations of time, with the authentic yellow lustre of antique gold.

: :   : :

He shut himself into the front passenger seat of the car, and held his head, because it felt as if it might burst if he worked the brain within it too hard. One little guinea in the sand of the tunnel, and a fistful of them in Morwenna's coffin. And the door locked, and both keys in police custody, and the whole thing impossible, unless— it was the last thing he had overheard as he retreated— unless there was yet another key.

Or another door! Nobody had said that, but he couldn't stop thinking it. Not an ordinary door, a very retiring door, one that wasn't easy to find.

Under the ground he'd had almost no sense of direction, but Dominic had said—somewhere under the dunes. Paddy took an imaginary bearing from the church towards the blow-hole under the Dragon's Head, and tried frantically to estimate distances. It was possible. It had to be possible, because there was no other possible way of accounting for everything.

They were down there a long time, nearly an hour. He stayed in the car all the time, because it had dawned on him that if he spied on them, or even asked them questions when they returned, he would have to tell them things in exchange; and he couldn't do that, not yet, not without other people's consent. No, there was only one thing to do, and that was go straight to the Pollards, and tell them what he knew, and try to make them see that the next move was up to them.

But there was no reason why he shouldn't use his eyes to the best advantage when the five men emerged from the deep enclosure of the Treverra tomb. Hewitt climbed the steps only to cross to his car, take a small rug from the boot, and make a second trip down into the vault with it. When he came up again he was carrying the rug rolled into a thick, short bundle under his arm. What was inside it, allowing for the bulk of the rug itself, might be about the size of a three-pound bag of flour, but seemed to be a good deal heavier. Say, a small gunnysack full of coins—or maybe a little leather draw-string bag, such as they used for purse and wallet in the eighteenth century. About the right size, at any rate, to match that small, shapeless bundle Rose had carried under her arm at noon.

Tim got into the car prepared for questions, and there were none. " Don't you want to know if it is really Morwenna?" he offered, concerned at such uncharacteristic continence.

" Well, yes, of course!" The boy brightened readily. " I thought you'd tell me what I'm allowed to know. I didn't want to poke my nose past where the line's drawn."

" Such virtue!" said Tim disapprovingly. " You're not sickening for something, are you?"

He started the engine, and the Mini came about gently in the trodden space before the church, and followed the police car back to the road.

" Is Uncle Simon riding with them, this time?"

" Yes, he wanted to talk to the pathologist. We're pretty sure it's Morwenna. Right age, right period, right build, no reason to suppose it would be anyone else. There'll be some work to do on fabric, and all that, but it looks authentic."

" Where are we going now?"

" Back to the police station. We've got a bit of conferring to do, if you wouldn't mind amusing yourself for an hour or so. Or would you rather I took you home first?"

" No," said Paddy, almost too quickly and alertly. " I'll come down into town with you, that'll suit me fine. While you're in your official huddle, there's somebody I want to see."

::   ::

He knocked at the front door of the second pink cottage in Cliffside Row just as the church clock was chiming half past seven; and on the instant he recoiled a step or two nervously, almost wishing he had let well alone, for the consequences of the knock manifested themselves before the door was opened. Something—it sounded like a glass— shattered on a quarried floor. A girl's voice uttered a small, frightened cry, and a young man's, suddenly sharp with fury and helplessness, shouted: " For God's sake, girl, what's up with you to-day? Anybody'd think a gun had gone off. It's only the door. If there's something wrong with you,

I wish you'd have the sense to tell me. Oh, come out!
I'll go."

The door, suddenly flung wide, vanished with startling
effect, as if Jim Pollard's large young fist had plucked it off.
Levelled brown eyes under a thick frowning ridge of brow
stared dauntingly at Paddy.

"Well, what's up?" The eyes, once they focused upon
him, knew him well enough. "Oh, it's you, young Rossall.
What do you want?" Less unfriendly, but as anxious as
ever to get rid of him and get back to whatever scene they
had been playing between them there in the doll's-house
living-room. The knock on the door had been only a
punctuation mark. Paddy felt small, unsupported, and
less certain of the sacred harmony of marriage than he had
been two minutes ago. But he'd started it, and now there
was no backing out.

"I'd like to talk to you and Rose, please. It's very
important."

"Mrs. Pollard to you, my lad," said Jim smartly. "All
right, come in."

"I'm sorry! She used to let me call her Rose, but I
won't do it if you don't like it. It was only habit."

He stepped over the brightly-Cardinalled doorstep into
the pretty toy room, and Jim closed the door behind him.
Rose, clattering dust-pan and brush agitatedly in the
minute kitchen beyond, was sweeping up the fragments of
the glass she had dropped. The door between was open,
and Paddy saw her slide a furtive glance at him, and take
heart. All the same, her eyes were evasive and her hands
unsteady when she came in.

"Hallo, Paddy, what's the matter?"

"Nothing with me," he said, making straight for the
essential issue, head-down and ready for anything. "It's
you! I came to tell you I know where you went this morning, and what you did. I saw you take something with you
into the Dragon's Hole, and I know where you left it.
Don't you see how silly it is to act as if you've done something bad, when you haven't? Mr. Pollard, you must get
her to tell the police everything, it's the best thing, really

it is. I know about the money and the jewellery, you see,
I know she put them——"

His impetuous rush had carried him thus far through a
silence of stupefaction on one side and desperation on the
other, but now, in a subdued way which didn't carry
beyond the walls, hell broke loose. Rose burst into tears
and flung herself face-down into a chair. Jim gaped open-
mouthed from one to the other of them, and with a muted
bellow of rage clouted Paddy on the ear with an open right
hand as hard as a spade. The blow slammed him back
against the wall, from which one of Rose's pretty little
calendar pictures, a golden-haired tot with a bunch of
forget-me-nots, promptly fell and smashed.

"You nasty little brat!" growled Jim through his teeth.
"You come here slandering my wife, and see what you'll
get! Who d'you think you're threatening with the police,
you——"

Nobody had ever hit Paddy like that before. Instead of
taming him it infuriated him. Clasping his smarting cheek,
he shouted back into the menacing face that leaned over
him: "I wasn't threatening her, I wasn't slandering her,
I said——"

"I heard what you said. Accusing her of taking money
and jewellery——"

"Don't be so bloody stupid!" yelled Paddy, blazing with
rage. "I never said she took them, I said she *put them
back*! Why the hell don't you listen?"

It was not language of which either his parents or his
teachers would have approved, but it stopped Jim, in the
act of loosing a damaging left at him, as though the breath
had been kicked out of him. His hands dropped. Shades
of doubt and consternation and suspicion pursued one
another over his candid face. Rose, through her desperate
sobs, implored indistinctly: "Don't hurt him, Jim! He
doesn't mean any harm."

Her husband turned and looked at her, quaking in the
frilly chair. "Now, look! There's one bloke around here
who doesn't seem to be in any of the secrets, and that's me.
And I'm going to know, and pretty sharpish, so you can

both make up your minds to that. Maybe what this kid's saying has got something in it, after all. The way you've been acting the last couple o' days, there could well be something queer going on, and you mixed up in it. If there is, I want to know. Now!"

His voice had worked its way down from the peak of anger to an intimidating quietness. He plucked Paddy away from the wall by the shoulders, and plumped him down hard in a chair.

"If I went off at half-cock, and you're being straight with me, I'm sorry, kid. But first I've got to know. Come on, let's have it. The lot. I've been trying to get some sense out of her for days, and she's been putting me off and swearing there was nothing, and going round like a dying duck in a thunder-storm. I'm about sick of it. If you know anything, let's have it, and know where we are."

Paddy took a deep breath, and told him everything he knew and everything he guessed. Rose, subsiding into exhausted silence, still hid her face.

"I came to tell you," said Paddy, with dignified indignation, "that I know very well you can't have done anything wrong, and it's dead silly to carry on as if you have. I don't know what's behind all this, but I do know you'll only get yourself into trouble if you go on hiding things. What you ought to do is go straight to the police, and tell them all you know. That's the only way to help yourself."

Jim took his hands from the boy, and looked down at Rose's heaving shoulders. There was hardly any need to ask, but he asked, all the same, his voice baffled and exasperated, and painfully gentle.

"Is that right, Rose, what he says? *Did* you——"

A fresh spurt of tears, but she scrubbed them away with the stoical determination of despair. "I had to get them out of the house. I didn't want you to know. It wasn't my fault, but it was even less yours, and I wanted you kept out of it."

"Go and wash your face and pretty yourself up," said Jim. "We're going to the police. Now." He turned to fix a stern but no longer unfriendly eye on Paddy. "All three of us," he said with emphasis.

:: ::

"Yes," said Rose, bolt upright and pale of face on one of Hewitt's hard chairs, "it's true, there is a way in. I'll show you. If somebody'd leaned against the right edge of the right stone, there in the vault, he'd have found it, only it's placed so nobody's likely to, not by accident. It's one of the facing slabs in the corner. It swivels on an iron bar that runs through it from top to bottom. I reckon they put it all in when the vault was made. It'll only swivel one way, and you'd have a job to find it from the tunnel side unless you know.

"And it's true, I did go there, like Paddy told you. I went and put the things back in the poor lady's grave—but I never took them in the first place. I wanted to give them back, and I didn't know how else to do it. I was going to put them loose in the vault, because I couldn't have shifted the stone. But she—she—you'd uncovered her. I saw her——" She put her hands up to her cheeks and drew breath in a single hysterical sob, her eyes fixed and horrified. Jim put his hand on her shoulder, and his index finger stroked her neck surreptitiously above the collar of the smart cotton shift-dress, with a quite unexpected tenderness. It calmed and eased her, reminding her of life. Death was a long way off, and she could make a good fight of it if events threatened her tenure or Jim's. She stooped her cheek to his hand fleetingly. They all saw it, and could not help being moved.

A nerve of awareness quivered in Paddy, and troubled his innocence, but the sensation was pleasurable and private, and he kept it to remember and ponder afterwards.

"How did you know about the tunnel and the entrance to the vault?" asked Hewitt, in the neutral tone he found so productive.

"My dad showed me."

"And how did he discover it?"

"I don't know. Accident, I suppose. He was a questing kind of man, he liked nosing things out. It was going to happen to somebody, sometime, and it just happened to be my dad. He never told me how it happened. But he found it. About three years ago, it would be. He began to bring home little things he hid, and in a small house it isn't easy to hide that you're hiding things. And I'm curious, too. I hunted for them, I found some gold buttons. I didn't know they were gold, not till he told me."

"You asked him about them then?"

"Yes, I did, but at first he wouldn't tell me anything. Then he got a bit above himself, and started showing me more things, a ring it was, once, and another time three gold coins. And then one day he made me go with him, and he took me and showed me the tunnel in the rock, and showed me how to get into the vault at the end of it. That was the first time I ever saw the coffins. He told me he'd got the stuff he was bringing out of the smaller one— the lady's coffin. I didn't want anything to do with it, I begged him to put them all back and leave them alone, but he never took any notice of anything I said. I was scared, but I didn't like to tell anyone, not on my own father. Even if there'd been anyone to tell, then," said Rose, simply, and fondled Jim's hand on her shoulder. "And there wasn't. Not close to me."

"Was he, do you know, disposing of any of these pieces he lifted out of the grave?"

"Yes, he began to. I think he didn't know how to go about it himself, but after a bit he took up with a fisherman who used to come after me, a queer fellow he was, name of Ruiz. Spanish he was, only way back. I mean, he'd always lived in Cornwall himself, and his folks, too. My dad started encouraging him, and wanted me to be nice to him, but I didn't like him much. He got to be quite a crony of Dad's, and that was queer, because he didn't have many. They used to knock about together quite a bit. I got to thinking maybe this Ruiz chap was shipping some of the things out abroad for him, because he knew a lot of people over there, in France and Spain, and he spoke the languages, too. They went on like that for about six months, and then they fell out. I think this here Ruiz

wanted a bigger share, and was threatening to give the
show away if he didn't get it."

"Did they talk about it in front of you?"

"No, only that one time, when they fell out, and then
it wasn't much. Ruiz flung off out of the house, and my
dad went after him, and they made it up. Anyway, they
came back together, and they had their heads together all
the rest of the evening, as thick as ever. But then a bit
later this Ruiz was drowned at sea. I don't know if you
remember, his boat never came back from fishing, one
blowy night. His body was washed up on the Mortuary
a few weeks later. Then I did hope my dad would give
up, not having anyone to sell the things for him, and I
think he did for nearly a year. But then he began to bring
things again, and started going off sometimes for a couple
of days at a time, and wouldn't tell me where he was
going."

"And where did you think he was going? You must have
had some ideas on the subject."

"Not about where, not exactly. But I did think he'd
started selling the things himself where he could, round
antique shops, and like that. I tried to get him to stop,
but he only told me not to be a fool. And by that time
Jim had started coming after me." She flushed warmly
even at the mention of his name. "We had a bit of a fight
for it, because Dad didn't want to lose his housekeeper.
But we did it in the end. And was I glad to get away to
a home of my own!"

Hewitt turned his pen placidly on the desk, regarding
her with his most benevolent and unrevealing face. "But
that didn't end it, did it?"

"It did, until about a week ago." She thought back,
biting her lip. "Last Monday it was—five days ago. Dad
came when Jim was out, and brought this whole bag of
coins, and some rings and things, all there was left. He
said so. He said to hide them and keep them for him.
I know I ought to have refused, but I was scared of him.
You can't just stop being scared of somebody," said Rose,
with unexpected directness and dignity, "when you have

been all your life. He said he'd take it out of Jim if I didn't do what he wanted. It seemed the easiest thing then to put them away out of sight till I could see my way. But then," she said, apprehensive eyes on Hewitt's face, "you came yesterday and told us he was dead. And I knew you were sending men to ask questions all over about Jim and me. I didn't know what to do, I was terrified you might search the house, and find those things there. I had to get rid of them, and the only thing that seemed even half-way right was to put them back where he took them from. And that's what I did. Only she—I never can forget it— seeing her——"

"You should have told me," said Jim reproachfully, "and not tried to do things by yourself, that way."

"Jim never knew anything about it until now. He never knew the things were in the house. And I never wanted them. I never wanted anything to do with it."

"All right, Rose! Now you've done what you should have done in the first place, and if ever you find yourself in a spot like that again, don't you run the risk of putting yourself under suspicion, you just come to me, and bring the whole thing into the open. Now there's one thing you can do to help us, as well as showing us the entrance into the vault. Can you remember any of the pieces your father brought home in all that time?"

"Yes, some I can," she said hopefully. "They were all that old, you know, they were different from the sort you see now."

"Well, when you go home, you try to make out a list of the ones you remember, and describe them as well as you can, so that we can try to find them again. Will you do that?"

"Yes, Mr. Hewitt, I'll try."

"And don't keep secrets from your husband from now on, if you want a peaceful life. All right! I may want to ask you some more questions to-morrow, for now we'll let you rest and think it over. Jim, I'd like you to go with her, Snaith will drive you down to the old church, and I'll follow in a few minutes and join you there. After that you can take her home and keep a strict eye on her, see she doesn't get into any more mischief."

"She won't," said Jim grimly, and twisted a finger furtively in her fair hair, and tweaked it tight.

On the way out, still holding his wife very possessively by the arm, he halted squarely in front of Paddy, and stood looking down dubiously but not particularly penitently at the print of his fingers on the boy's swollen cheek and ear. The kid looked tired, dazed, battered but content. Large eyes stared back just as appraisingly, withholding judgment but assessing quality. They liked each other. They liked each other very well. True, Paddy did burn for one moment in the dread that Jim would blurt out an apology for the clout, and call everyone's attention to it; but he should have known better.

"Thanks, mate!" said Jim calmly. "I'll give you as fair a chance, some day, and we'll get even."

"That's all right, mate," said Paddy, wooden-faced, and eyeing the precise spot at the angle of Jim's jaw where ideally he should connect. "And I'll take it."

"Come three or four years," observed Jim, looking him over critically, " I reckon you'll be about ready, too." There wasn't much muscle on the light body yet, but he had a nice long reach, and speed, and spirit enough for an army.

"I reckon so," said Paddy; and with mutual respect they parted.

:: :: :: ::

A concerted sigh of relaxation and wonder and speculation went round the room as soon as the door had closed, and the sound of feet descending the stairs had ebbed to a distant, lingering echo. They stirred and rose, drawing together round the desk.

"You believe her story?" asked Simon.

"Yes, I believe it. All of it, maybe, most of it, certainly. Maybe Jim's clever enough to put over an act of knowing nothing about it, but I don't think so."

"He didn't know," said Paddy, standing up in the middle of events with authority, for hadn't he precipitated this single-handed? "They were rowing when I got there, before I ever got in the house. She was all nerves and cried if he looked at her, and he was just about frantic trying to get sense out of her. Why should he act when there was nobody else there?"

"I'm prepared to accept that," agreed Hewitt benevolently. "Rose has cleared up quite a number of things for us, but she hasn't shed any light on who killed her father. There's nothing to put Jim out of the running for that, so far."

"He didn't know about the tunnel into the vault," said Paddy doggedly, "so he couldn't have put him there."

"Oh, yes, he could, laddie. Finding a back way in doesn't block the front door. There was a key almost anyone could get at. There could be others who knew about the back door, too, of course. Don't worry, I wouldn't say Jim makes a good suspect, but he isn't out of it. We've got plenty to do yet—looking into Trethuan's finances, for one thing."

He reached for his hat, smothering a yawn. "Well, I'll be off down and take a look at Rose's swivelling stone. Care to come along?"

"Not me," said Tim firmly, after a quick glance at his son. "Paddy and I are off home."

Paddy wasn't really sorry. He'd had enough excitement for one day, and a mere hole in the wall isn't so wonderful, once located. Secret tunnels sound fine, but they're two-a-penny wherever there was organised smuggling a couple of hundred years ago, whether on a sporting or a commercial scale. It would keep. He went down the stairs after the others, Tim's arm about his shoulders.

"Well, at any rate," said Simon, as they emerged into the faint, starry, salty coldness of after-summer and not-yet-autumn, "we do know now what Trethuan was acting so cagey about, why he didn't want the tomb opened."

"Do we?" said George Felse.

"Don't we? With all that stuff there to be found——"

"Ah, but it wasn't there. There was nothing there this morning but the body—remember? He must have made a special journey, last Sunday, and taken away all that was left of Morwenna's treasure. At any rate, on Monday he gave it to Rose to hide for him. Once that was done, what was there to betray him? No one would know he'd been stealing it, no one would ever know it had been there at all. Oh, no," said George pensively, "we haven't found out yet why Trethuan was so mad to keep you out. It certainly wasn't because of Mrs. Treverra's money and jewels, removing them was no problem. They were a good deal more portable than the—purely hypothetical, of course, —brandy. No, the most puzzling thing about that little hoard is something quite different."

They had halted beside the cars. "Such as what?" asked Simon.

"Such as : What was it doing there in the first place?"

"That's it! That's it exactly! The way it looks," sighed Hewitt, sliding into the driving seat, "no one ever told Mrs. Treverra that you can't take it with you."

CHAPTER IX

SUNDAY AFTERNOON

DOMINIC CAME DOWN to lunch in his best suit, and with a demure gait to match, threaded his way between the tables in the bar, and slid on to the stool next to his mother's, in the approved casual manner.

"Dry Martini, please, Sam."

"Darling, you *have* come on!" said Bunty admiringly. "You even sound as if you expect to get it."

"Careful, now!" cautioned Sam, with a face so straight that apart from the moustache it was practically featureless. "That vermouth's powerful stuff." He spared a moment, in spite of the noon rush of business after church, to admire his young guest's grave Sabbath appearance. "I hear you've got old Hewitt coming to lunch."

Dominic centred the knot of his tie more severely. "This won't stay on past two o'clock, if it lasts that long. But it's the least I could do. After all, Dad did put on a collar and tie for me, the night we got to know Simon and the Rossalls. Not unprompted," he added, looking down his nose into his glass.

"Look who's talking!" said Bunty. "Twelve minutes ago he looked like something a water spaniel had dragged in off the beach. If anyone gets the credit for his present appearance, it should be me."

"Well, congratulations, Mrs. Felse," said Sam reverently, "it's very, very beautiful."

Dominic began to get down from his stool with great dignity, but not so purposefully as to suggest that he had any real intention of leaving. "Look, I'll go away if I'm cramping your style at all."

"Leave the glass," said Bunty accommodatingly, "I'll take care of it."

"You touch it!" He took care of it jealously himself, spreading both elbows more comfortably. Through the windows that overlooked the terrace, half-empty to-day because the wind was in the wrong quarter and the sunny air deceptively cool, they saw George and Hewitt approaching in earnest conversation.

"They're here. Good, I'm hungry. And, Sam, talking of powerful stuff, don't you think you could find us a drop of the real McCoy to go with the coffee? The special, for Mr. Hewitt. I think you really should offer it with the compliments of the house."

"I might, at that," said Sam, grinning.

"And serve it yourself. Just to show your conscience is clear."

"My conscience is always clear. I've got it properly trained."

"I bet you you daren't," said Dominic, glittering with mischief.

"You bet me what I daren't?"

"The price of the brandy."

"Plus duty?"

"Oh, have a heart!" protested Dominic, injured.

Bunty slid from her stool and shook out the peacock-blue skirt that made her chestnut hair take fire in opposition. "I hate to admit an impediment to this marriage of true minds, but I'm not really sure that this is the right time to tease Detective-Sergeant Hewitt. Are you both sure of your alibis? He might have a warrant in his pocket right now."

George and Hewitt were already entering the doorway. Sam watched them approach, his face benign and childlike. Apart, of course, from the whiskers. Those whiskers, Dominic reflected, must be worth a fortune to him.

"Don't you worry," he said, momentarily serious, "the old boy knows all about my alibi long ago. He may look stolid, it's his stock-in-trade, but there isn't much he misses. I'm checked up on and passed harmless, that's for sure, or we should have seen more of him around."

"Well, hang it," said Dominic, "I was one of the blokes trying to pull the victim *out* of the sea. Everybody knows where *I* was."

"That could be very good cover for anyone who'd just thrown him in," pointed out Bunty darkly, and took her son firmly by the elbow. "Come on, we have a guest. Put your company face on."

"It is on," he said indignantly.

"It's crooked, then. Straighten it."

::   ::

Sam appeared at Bunty's shoulder with the coffee, beaming and benign, and distributed the delicate, tall-stemmed balloons he kept for special occasions.

"With the compliments of the house, Mr. Felse," he said ceremoniously, catching George's inquiring eye, and began to pour the brandy with reverence.

"That's very handsome of you, Sam," George acknowledged civilly. He looked at Bunty, and her face was limpid and innocent. He looked at Dominic, and his was pleased and bland.

"Not at all," deprecated Sam, rubbing thumb and forefinger together gleefully at Dominic from behind Hewitt's back. Dominic remained seraphic, flattered and serene, just artful enough to retain a pinch of the schoolboy in his impersonation of the man-of-the-world. It didn't fool George. But good brandy is good brandy.

"What is it, Sam, a drop of special?"

"My own favourite," said Sam fondly and truthfully, and judiciously withdrew the bottle, leaving only a very modest dose in Dominic's glass. That should have shaken the practised calm, if anything could, but Dominic merely flicked one glance at Sam, unreadable to the others, and contained his displeasure to loose it at a more opportune time. His small, delighted smile never wavered for an instant. "Give me your opinion, Mr. Hewitt, I know you're a good judge."

Hewitt caressed and warmed the glass in his large palms, and let his nose enjoy itself. "Lovely bouquet, Sam! Not a trace of that overtone of brass you sometimes get."

"That's just what I like about it," said Sam, feelingly. "I'm glad to have my judgment confirmed by an expert. You don't mind if I quote you, Mr. Hewitt? Try the flavour, you won't be disappointed."

Hewitt tried it, and was not disappointed. One heavy eyelid lifted from the happy contemplation of his glass, one round, bright eye examined Sam minutely, shifted from him to Dominic, and lingered thoughtfully. Dominic retired coyly into his glass, but slanted one glance across it, so quickly that it should have slid harmlessly by. Hewitt winked. Dominic looked down his nose and appeared to have noticed nothing unorthodox. Honours were approximately even.

"That's lovely stuff, Sam. You go on buying it as long as it's on offer, that's all the advice I can give you."

"I will, Mr. Hewitt, glad to know it has your approval."

It was a pity that Mrs. Shubrough should have to loom up at that moment from the direction of the bar, and strike the one discordant note: "Telephone for you, Mr. Hewitt. It's Mr. Rackham calling from the police station. He says it's very important."

The little bubble of comedy burst damply round them. They watched the stocky figure shoulder its way out through the glass doors, and they were back with an unsolved double murder.

"I feel cheap," announced Dominic, after a moment of self-examination.

"Don't be self-important," said George witheringly. "You don't think fate's got time to cast a disapproving eye on your little capers, do you? Besides, you don't feel cheap at all, you only feel you ought to. Now if you want to make yourself useful, take your mother out for the afternoon, because I suspect I shall be out of circulation. And kick up your heels all you want—there won't be any nemesis listening to you. Nemesis has got more important things to do."

: :   : :

"I've had two men out since Friday," said Hewitt, slowing at the beginning of the steep drop into the town, "looking for the dentist who put in all that work on our unidentified corpse's teeth. Rackham's found him. At least, it seems likely it's the right fellow, but he's a cautious one, won't say for sure from the charts. Wants to see the molars before he commits himself, but is sure he'll know his own work again if it is the bloke he thinks."

"If he's as cagey as that," said George, "I take it he's naming no names yet. Where did your man find him? Evidently he isn't a Maymouth man."

"Plymouth. Just got back with him."

"What sort of a fellow is he? I hope he knows what he's going to see."

"Small, dapper and highly-strung," said Hewitt, "according to Rackham. He'll be all right. It's the big, husky ones that keel over." He turned into the square, almost deserted at this hour on a fine Sunday, the old-fashioned shop-fronts gated, shuttered and still. "Well, if we can't do much on the Trethuan case until to-morrow, maybe we can get somewhere on this other one. Didn't have more in his deposit account or in the house—Trethuan, I mean—than you could account for as a careful man's savings, but I fancy he's got a lot put away somewhere in cash from this antique traffic of his. Maybe in a safe-deposit box somewhere, maybe under the floor-boards at home. We haven't been over the house properly yet. It'll be somewhere. And we'll find it. As far as we can tell, all of the stuff that he hadn't already disposed of piecemeal, we've got in custody. Rose has identified what we've got, and furnished us with a nice little list of things he brought home earlier. We should be able to trace some of them through the trade. Here we are! Don't come down to the mortuary with us unless you want to, George. You've had all that once."

"I can stand it. I might learn something. I like to hear an expert on his own subject."

Rackham was a deceptively simple-looking young local man, fresh-faced and bright. Beside his cheerful, extrovert bulk the dentist from Plymouth looked meagre and unreal, and as highly-strung as his companion had indicated, but a second and narrower look corrected the impression. He was wiry, durable and sharply competent, and he had come armed with all his relevant records and charts, ready to go into extreme detail. So firmly astride his hobby-horse, he was not to be thrown by any corpse, however fragmentary, provided its jaw was still intact. In the chill basement mortuary he probed, matched and demonstrated in complete absorption; and at the end of his examination he snapped the rubber band back into place round his records, and declared himself satisfied, and prepared to swear to the dead man's identity in court as soon as it might be required of him.

"I was practically certain from the charts your man brought with him, but it was essential that I should see the work for myself. Yes, it's mine. I can give you dates for the whole sequence of treatments. They went on for about eight weeks in the spring of 1961, and occasionally we had to adjust the appointments because of his sea trips. He should have come back to me for a check-up six months later, but he never came. That does happen, of course, it needn't mean anything. But it could mean that by then he couldn't come. He was a fisherman, and he gave me a Maymouth address—I've got it here in the records. His name," said the little man blithely, unaware that he was springing a land-mine, "was Walter Ruiz."

: :   : :

"On the face of it," fretted Hewitt, prowling the length of his small office like a restive tiger, "it's damned impossible. Walter Ruiz is buried in St. Mary's churchyard, up the town, with a stone over him to prove it. There was an inquest, and he was identified."

"He's just been identified again," said George dryly. "Very impressively, for my money. It seems that one or the other of two equally positive identifications must be mistaken. The question is, which?"

"You heard him. That amount of dental work in one course of treatment, fully documented as such things have never been before, coupled with the individual formation of the bones, and all the rest of it, makes this man's jaw about as unique as a set of finger-prints. That evidence would stand up at any inquest."

"But so did something else, presumably something that looked equally sound, at the previous inquest. According to what Rose told us last night, Ruiz and his boat failed to come home after fishing in rough weather, and his body was washed up on the Mortuary a few weeks later. A few weeks in the sea don't make a body any easier to identify, even a landsman knows that. But somebody did identify this one. Who was it? His parents? A brother? His wife? But no, he didn't have a wife, he came courting Rose, and her father wanted her to be nice to him. Her father found him useful, until he got a bit too demanding, and knew a bit too much."

Hewitt came back to his desk, and stood gazing at George across its empty surface for a long, dubious minute of silence.

"If you're trying to put ideas in my head, George, you're too late. They're there already." He reached out a large hand, and picked up the telephone, and with deliberation began to dial.

"I'm trying to sort out the ones I've got in mine," said

George. "It looks as if we're both being driven on the same shore. Did he have any family? It seems to me that a solitary like himself would be most likely to appeal to Trethuan as an ally, if he found it expedient to look round for one at all."

"You're so right, Ruiz didn't have any family. You're neck and neck with me, George." His head came up alertly as the burr of the telephone was answered. "Hallo, Henry! This is Tom Hewitt. Sorry to interrupt your Sunday nap, but I need a quick reference to something about two and a half years back, and you're the quickest and most infallible referee in town. Nip down to your files and look it up for me, will you? You probably know the answer, but look it up anyhow, I want to have it officially. An inquest on a seaman drowned and cast up on the Mortuary, I think it will be in March or April, 1962. Name of Walter Ruiz. A routine job, it seemed at the time. But now I want to know *who identified him*. Just that. Call me back as soon as you can. And thanks very much!"

He hung up, laying the receiver so softly in its cradle that there was no sound to break the slight tension in the room. He sat down gently and folded his hands, and looked at George.

"No family. No brothers, no sisters. There was his widowed mother, up to about seven years ago, I remember. They had a cottage down the south end of the sea front. After she died he lived alone, kept himself to himself, and bothered nobody. The excise people did have their suspicions of him, though not, I think, over the occasional drop of brandy. He was never actually caught out over anything. Just another lone wolf. If he needed hands he took on casuals, and dropped them again afterwards. Nobody ever worked with him regularly. Nobody was ever in his confidence."

"That was your local paper?" Local papers are formidable institutions. They may ignore national events, but they must get every name right, and every date, and every detail, within their own field. "Proprietor? Editor? Or both?"

"Both. Henry still lives above his own offices, he won't be long looking it up, his files are kept in apple-pie order. I could," admitted Hewitt, "have got the same information at least three other ways, but not so quickly."

It was barely a quarter of an hour before the telephone rang. Hewitt lifted it out of its cradle before it could cough out a second call. He listened for a moment with an unreadable face. "Thank you, Henry! That's exactly what I wanted to know. I'm very grateful. Good-bye!" he replaced the instrument, and sat looking at George.

"The body that came up on the Mortuary and was buried as Walter Ruiz was identified by the man who was considered to be his closest, maybe his only, friend. Zebedee Trethuan."

::   ::

It accounted for everything. They sat and looked at it, and details of Rose's story fell into place like bits of a jigsaw puzzle, filling in what had seemed, until this morning, the most mysterious third of the whole picture.

"Well, I know now which identification I'd trust," said Hewitt with curious mildness, pacing the room again, but with a longer, easier stride. "A handy and unrecognisable corpse turns up on the Mortuary, and you have need of just that to lay a ·ghost. The ghost of someone known to have been associated with you, and now missing, supposedly drowned at sea. How nice and easy to say this is it, and get it put away under a stone with your man's name on it, so that no one will ever start asking awkward questions. Walter Ruiz is dead and buried respectably, and everybody knows it. Everything beautifully tidy and safe. And then this interfering Simon Towne comes along, and puts it into the old lady's mind, of all crazy things, to *open the Treverra tomb*!"

A cool voice from the doorway said deprecatingly: "I'm afraid he's interfering again. I'm sorry, I did knock."

They both swung round in surprise. So intent had they been on their revelation and its implications that they had failed to hear Simon's light feet climbing the stairs. He stood in the doorway, eyebrows cocked obliquely, smiling a little. "The desk sergeant told me I could come up. Don't blame him, I told him I had something that might be relevant to tell you. I really did knock, but you didn't hear me. And I was just in time to hear no good of myself. Would you rather I waited downstairs?"

"No, that's all right, Mr. Towne, come in. You might as well hear the context as well," said Hewitt good-humouredly. "I wasn't calling you interfering on my own account, it was what you might call an imaginative projection. Come in, and close the door."

"I seem to have missed a lot." Simon hitched a knee over the corner of the desk, and looked from one to the other of them, frowning. "Did I hear you talking about Ruiz? That's the fellow Rose Pollard talked about last night, the one who was shipping pieces of jewellery abroad for her father? What's he got to do with the Treverra tomb? I thought he was buried in St. Mary's churchyard."

"So did everybody else, Mr. Towne, except one person, the one who knew he was somewhere very different. In Jan Treverra's coffin, where we found him."

"*We found him*?" Simon drew breath sharply, and flashed a doubtful glance at George. "This is serious? Then you're telling me that the unidentified one—the one underneath—*that* is *Ruiz*? But they wouldn't bury a man under that name without good authority. Someone must have vouched for him."

"Someone did. He came up practically naked and featureless, after six weeks in the sea. What could be better? The man who'd put the real Walter Ruiz in Treverra's coffin, where he hoped he'd lie uninvestigated till doomsday, jumped at his chance when it offered, and got another body buried as Ruiz, publicly and decently. And that would have been the end of it, if you hadn't conceived this notion of finding out whether Treverra really did have his poems buried with him. Imagine how this fellow would feel when he heard it! Wasn't it enough to make him frantic? Wasn't it enough to account for his threatening you, pestering you, trying to frighten you off? Anything to get you to go away and leave well alone."

Open-mouthed, eyes huge and blank with astonishment, Simon whispered : "Trethuan?"

"Who else? Doesn't it make sense of everything? He got Ruiz to help him dispose of the valuables he'd been steadily lifting from Mrs. Treverra's coffin, they were partners for about six months, so Rose says. Then they quarrelled, and she thinks Ruiz was demanding a bigger share of the proceeds, maybe threatening to make trouble if he didn't get it. And shortly after that Ruiz's boat vanished one night, and never came back and Ruiz was presumed drowned. And the next possible and unidentifiable body that came up on the Mortuary—Trethuan identified it as Ruiz. Isn't it plain what his reason must have been?"

"It looks," said George, "as if Trethuan killed him either actually in the vault, or very close to it, maybe in the rock tunnel. Why else hide him there? He was a big man. Admittedly Trethuan was a pretty powerful person, too, but he wouldn't want to move the body any farther than necessary. The sea was close, but the sea was no good. Ruiz had a skull fractured by repeated blows. No passing that off as the work of the sea. A drowned man, like Trethuan himself later, is another matter."

"I see two possibilities," said Hewitt. "Either Ruiz pretended to be reconciled, and then spied on Trethuan on his next trip, confronted him in the act, and was killed —for you can bet your last bob a man like Trethuan would want to keep the source entirely to himself and Rose, he'd never willingly let his partner into the secret. Or else—and perhaps this is the more likely—Trethuan pretended to agree to whatever Ruiz wanted, offered to prove his good faith by showing him where their profits were coming from, and took him there with the fixed intention of killing him and hiding him there. If he'd looked in the lady's coffin, he'd looked in Treverra's, too, he wouldn't miss anything. He knew the coffin was empty. He supplied it with a body."

"Could it be done by one man alone?" asked George, and turned his head and looked at Simon.

"Yes, it could. One man couldn't possibly get either

of the stones off and replace it again unbroken. But he could prise it sidelong, all right. Enough to probe inside. Enough to dump a man inside, and cover him again——"
He drew breath in a deep gasp, realising the full implications of what he was saying. He sat voiceless and motionless, his eyes blank and colourless as glass, staring inward at his own imaginings.

"It could be done, all right," said Hewitt. "Trethuan did it repeatedly, didn't he? Morwenna's stone is lighter than the other, that one he must have shifted whenever he went back for another raid, enough to get his arm down into the poor thing's belongings. The other, presumably, he moved only twice, once when he made his assay and found the coffin empty, once when he filled it."

"There was still the boat to dispose of," said George.

"That wouldn't be any problem. Trethuan was an amphibian like all the rest of Maymouth. His folks were fishermen. He had a dinghy of his own. To scuttle Ruiz's boat by night and get back to land safely wouldn't cause him much trouble. You don't have to go far off this coast to find deep water. And he had time. Ruiz lived alone, nobody was going to raise a hue and cry immediately he didn't come home to supper. We'll go through all the circumstances again. We'll find out who first called attention to the fact that he hadn't come in from fishing. And when. It may even have been a couple of days later, time enough to wait for a pretty blowy night."

"And wouldn't there be a certain risk in rushing to claim a corpse, like that?" suggested George. "Suppose he said it was Ruiz, and then somebody else really did recognise it—by a ring, or something?"

"Ah, but he didn't rush! He was canny. He waited for one nobody else was claiming. Henry tells me—it wasn't my department—the police had been appealing for help in identifying that body for several days before he stepped in. And even then, if it had been obviously the wrong height or age, or shape, he only had to let well alone and say no, I don't know him. No, he had everything sewed up.

And he lay low with his thefts for a year or so, and left the stuff where he thought it was safest, before he started hawking pieces round the buyers in this country. And then you came along, Mr. Towne, and heaved a brick through all his plans and precautions. Nobody'd ever shown any interest in the tomb before. He made haste to shift the rest of the valuables, but he was terrified to move the body. No wonder he tried all he dared to scare you off. He knew it wouldn't pass for Treverra, once the scholars and antiquaries got their noses into it."

Simon lifted a dazed face from between his hands, and stared before him. George had not noticed until this minute the blue rings under his eyes, the copper shadows hollowing his lean cheeks. He might not have noticed even now, if he had not possessed knowledge acquired by the accident of being with Phil Rossall on the evening of Paddy's disappearance. Not everybody had reason to see beyond the bright, handsome public image of Simon Towne to the marginal failures and deprivations that crippled his private progress.

"Look, do you really mean to say that whoever killed Trethuan took him in there, and dumped him into the coffin with—*the man he himself had killed*?" He said this very slowly and deliberately, as if his lips were stiff, and had to be driven to form the syllables.

"That's exactly what I mean to say." Hewitt was triumphant. "I haven't the slightest doubt that that's what happened. And a supreme bit of irony it is!"

"A supreme bit of cheek!" said Simon furiously. "If I wrote that and published it, I'd be hooted out of journalism. Nobody, not even a novelist, could get away with a bare-faced coincidence like that."

"Not a coincidence at all," Hewitt objected brusquely. "There were completely logical reasons why Ruiz should be disposed of precisely there, and in that way. As we've demonstrated. And there'll be equally logical causes leading to the precise effect we're left with, the presence of Trethuan's body in the same hiding-place. Don't forget there's a waste of sand all round it. Don't forget that a stone coffin is good cover. But I grant you we've still got to find out what the precise causes were in Trethuan's case. He drowned in the sea, that's definite. He was taken dead into the vault. Why, and how, we don't know yet. It may have been through the door, with one of the two keys. Or it may have been through the tunnel. If young Paddy really saw him in the water about half past five, then the body might well be brought ashore on the Mortuary after the next high tide. He might be cast up fairly close to St. Nectan's. And anyone who didn't know the vault was going to be opened might still think it a pretty safe hiding-place."

"There couldn't have been many who didn't know," said Simon. "I advertised my intentions loudly enough, for obvious reasons."

"Well, that's just one of the things we shall have to look into. That case remains. But this one is as good as closed. A few details to fill in, some back history to verify, but I'm in no doubt of the result myself. It's kind of tantalising," he said thoughtfully, "to know the middle of a story, and not the beginning or the end."

"That'll come, all in good time," said Simon, rising. He felt through his pockets for a crumpled packet of cigarettes, and offered them, and again began to search for matches. "Lord, I'm forgetting what I came for!" It was some small object at the bottom of his trouser pocket that had reminded him. He fished it out, a tiny, folded square of tissue paper.

"Paddy forgot to mention this last night, what with all the excitement, and to-day he's on duty, Tim being his own cowman on Sundays. I said I'd bring it in to you. They found it yesterday in the tunnel, not far from the entrance into the vault."

He leaned across to the lighter George was offering, and drew in smoke deeply and gratefully before he completed the unwrapping of the minute thing, and held it out on his open palm. A thin, broken gold ring, bent a little out of its true circle, the two ends pulled apart about a quarter of an inch. Hewitt took it up between finger and thumb, and stood staring at it warily, as though it might close on him and bite.

"I don't suppose it means a thing," said Simon apologetically, "but I said I'd deliver it, and I have. Can I run you back to the Dragon, George? It's on my way."

"Mr. Towne!" Hewitt had threaded the ring on the tip of his large brown forefinger, and was still gazing at it, a small, smug flare of pleasure in his eyes. "Where did you say this was found?"

"In the tunnel from the Dragon's Hole to the vault. Only about twenty yards from the vault end, Paddy says, but I daresay he can show you the exact spot. Tamsin actually found it. Does it matter?"

"The spot where this was found may very well be the actual spot where Ruiz was killed," said Hewitt happily, "that's all. It happens to be the identical twin to the one ring he's still wearing in his left ear."

CHAPTER X

SUNDAY NIGHT

ON THEIR WAY up through the quiet Sunday reaches of the town they passed the narrow opening of Church Street, and Simon suddenly braked hard as they overshot it, and began to reverse along the empty road.

"You don't mind a few more minutes' delay, George? I suddenly thought I'd like to have a look at the other fellow's grave, the one who isn't Walter Ruiz." He slowed the car beside the small lunette of gravel at the churchyard gate. The young lime trees, leaves just ripening into the yellower green of autumn, leaned over them.

"A sad sort of end he had," said Simon, threading the maze of little paths between the graves, "dying solitary in the sea, and then cast up here among humankind again, only to be used as a pawn in a dirty game, and have another man's name wished on him for all time. That's the sort of ghost I'd expect to haunt us. Somebody we've deprived even of his identity. After all, he was a man, too, somebody may have loved him, he may have had children. Suddenly he seems to me the most injured of all. I'd like just to see what they gave him to last him till doomsday. You did say there was a stone?"

"Hewitt said so. I wondered who paid for it."

"I wonder, too. Where do you suppose he'd be? It's a burial only two and a half years old. I should think that would be in the new part."

They passed by the vestry door, and the Vicar came out in his cassock, and joined them as naturally as one stream joins another. He had the hymn-board for the evening service in one hand, and a fistful of numbers in the other, and went on placidly slotting them into their places as he walked.

"Dan, you're just the man we need," said Simon. "We're looking for a grave. The man you buried as Walter Ruiz, a couple of years or so ago."

"You're heading the wrong way, then," said the Vicar tranquilly, neither missing nor acknowledging the doubt thus cast on the recorded identity, as though it did not matter one way or the other. "He was a seaman, we made room for him among the older graves, where all the mid-nineteenth-century sailors are. I thought he'd be more at home. This way!"

He led them, skirts fluttering round his Great-Dane strides, along a thread-like path swept darker in the high grass, to a remote corner in the angle of the stone wall, shaded with thorn trees.

"235," read Simon aloud, deciphering the numbers on the hymn-board upside-down. "Abelard's hymn. Maybe I should come to church to-night."

"Maybe you should, but don't expect me to tell you so."

"You won't believe this, but I used to sing in the choir. Alto. I could sing alto before my voice broke, and after.

I still can, it's a technique I was somehow born with. There's a splendid alto to ' *O Quanta Qualia* '." He began to sing it, softly, mellifluously, afloat above the pitch of his own true baritone speaking voice, and in Latin.

> " ' Vere Jerusalem est illa civitas,
>   Cuius pax iugis et summa iucunditas,
>   Ubi non praevenit rem desiderium,
>   Nec desiderio minus est premium.'

Wish and fulfilment can severed be ne'er, nor the thing prayed for come short of prayer ! That always seemed to me the most perfect of all definitions of heaven. But then, look who wrote it, poor devil ! He knew all about wish and non-fulfilment, and things falling short."

"Simon," said the Vicar, "I don't know whether I really ought to admire you for it, but you must be the only fellow I ever met with the effrontery to think of Abelard as a poor devil. Here you are, here's——" He had been about to say " Walter Ruiz "; instead he said, courteously but serenely : " —the man you're looking for."

A low, cropped grave, turfed over within a granite kerb, under the bough of a hawthorn tree. Grey old stones, seamed with fine viridian moss, leaning all round. A plain pillow stone at the head of the small enclosure, and inscribed on it :

> WALTER RUIZ
> Born May 8th, 1929,
> Drowned, March, 1962.
> " I will bring my people again
>   from the depths
>   of the sea."

"He wasn't Ruiz, you know," said Simon, standing gazing down at it with a shadowed face. "Nobody'll ever know now who he really was. I don't know why, but I feel bad about that. Even if we could think of him by a

name, and a face, and say: Poor old Smith, three years
next month since he was washed up!—even that would
be something, give him a place to exist in, a dimension in
which he'd be real. But now he's nobody."

"He's as surely somebody," said the Vicar placidly, "as
you are. And nothing could be much surer than that."

"But who? Doesn't that matter?"

"It matters who. It doesn't matter that we should know
who. He's been identified," said the Vicar, tucking his
hymn-board under his arm, "a long time ago, in the
only way that matters in the least now. And by a witness
who doesn't make mistakes."

"Yes—I see your point. 'I will bring my people again
from the depths of the sea.' Yes, he might have done
worse. Who provided the stone? You?"

"It's always been the tradition that the dead from the
sea, who had no families here to bury them, should be
a charge on the church. Look round you, if you think
a foreign name makes a man a stranger here."

They looked. Half the sea-faring nations of the west lay
there quietly enough together, with the scent of the salt
shore for ever in the wind that stirred the pale grasses
over them. Edvard Kekonnen, seaman. Hugh O'Neill,
master-mariner. Alfonso Nuñez, master-mariner. Vassilis
Kondrakis, seaman. Two Spanish shipmates, unknown by
name. Sean MacPeake, master-mariner. Jean Plouestion,
fisherman. Walter Ruiz, or X, fisherman, seaman or master-
mariner. "I will bring my people again from the depths of
the sea." It didn't much matter if no one else knew what
to call them, the voice they were listening for would have
all their names right.

"Yes," said Simon, a small, wry smile curling the corners
of his mouth, "this is the point of departure for a good
many heavens, seemingly, Valhalla, Tir-nan-Og, the lot.
It's the sea-going men who made the western islands heaven,
I suppose." He slipped into song again, very softly:

> "'Far the cloudless sky stretches blue
>   Across the isle, green in the sunlight.'

It sounds like Jan Treverra himself designing that paradise, doesn't it?

> *'There shall thou and I wander free*
> *On sheen-white sands, dreaming in starlight'.''*

" I was thinking much the same thing," agreed George, smiling. " What was it Dom said about your two epitaphs, that first evening we were up at the Place with you? Something about making the after-life sound like a sunshine cruise to the Bahamas."

Simon had begun to turn back towards the gravelled walk, his hands deep in his pockets, the air of the Hebridean song still soft and sweet in his mouth. He halted suddenly, stiffening; for a moment he hung perfectly still, then he turned a face sharp and pale beneath its gold with contained excitement.

" Dom said *what*? Would you mind saying that again?"

" He said the Treverra epitaphs made the after-life sound like a sunshine cruise to the Bahamas. Why? What nerve did that prick?"

" The nerve it should have pricked then, if I'd been even half awake. And I was there?" he protested furiously. " I heard this? And I didn't connect?"

" You laughed. Like the rest of us," said George, patient but mystified.

" I would! The fate of many another pregant utterance in its time. Why do I never listen properly to anyone but myself? My God, but I see now how it all began, all the first part of the story. You only have to put one bit in place, and all the other pieces begin to slide in and settle alongside. George, come to the Place to-night, will you? We're dining with the old lady, because Paddy has to go back to school to-morrow. Bring Bunty and Dominic, and come to coffee afterwards. You, too, Dan, please. I'd like you to be there."

" With pleasure," said the Vicar equably, " if you want me."

" I do. I want you all, everyone who was involved in this

investigation from the beginning. Because I can see my way now," said Simon, suddenly shivering in the chilling air of early evening and the tension of his own incandescent excitement. " I believe I can clear up the strange, sad case of Jan and Morwenna, the mystery that set off all these other mysteries. And I will, to-night."

: :   : :

They gathered round the long table in Miss Rachel's library, ten of them. The curtains were drawn, and the tide, already well past its height, lashed and cried with subsiding force off the point, in the soft, luminous dark. Miss Rachel sat at the head of the table, dispensing coffee royally and happily, with Paddy at her left because she would not let him out of her reach now that he was regained in good condition and angelic humour, and had forgiven her freely under the pretence of being freely forgiven. On her right, Simon, curiously quiet and strained and bright. Tamsin moved about the foot of the table handing coffee-cups, helped by Dominic. George and Bunty on one side of the table, Tim and Phil and the Vicar on the other. It was a long time since the old lady had assembled such a satisfactory court, she didn't even seem to mind that it was turning out to be Simon's court rather than hers. The more he disclaimed it, the more honestly he abdicated, the more surely this evening belonged to him.

" I wasn't the one who put my finger on the spot," he was saying with passionate gravity. " That was Dominic. I had to have my nose rubbed in the truth before I could even realise it was there."

" Me?" said Dominic, staggered. " I didn't do anything, how on earth did I get in on the credits?"

" You took one look at the Treverra epitaphs, and put your finger on the one significant thing about them. ' They make heaven sound like a sunshine cruise to the Bahamas,' you said."

" Did I? It must have been just a joke, then. I didn't see anything significant."

" You did, though you may not have realised it or taken it seriously. All that pretty verse about year-long summer, and golden sands, and sapphire seas—you saw intuitively what it really meant, and that it was very much this side the grave. Whether you ever examined what you knew or not, you offered it to me, and I didn't have the wit to look at it properly, and learn from it."

They saw now, dimly, where he was leading them. They sat still, all eyes upon Simon. His thin, long hands were linked on the table before him. The cigarette he had lighted and forgotten smoked slowly away to a cylinder of ash in the ashtray beside him. The tension that held them all silent and motionless proceeded from him, but only he seemed unaware of it.

" If ever there was a crazy bit of research, this was it. There we were, with Treverra's own tomb—well, not empty, but empty of the man who should have been in it, and his wife's coffin unhappily not empty, but most tragically occupied, by the poor lady who had died there, and, as we found out afterwards, by a pretty large sum in old money and jewels. This crazy, sad puzzle, and those two epitaphs for clues, and nothing else.

" You remember Treverra was the adored leader of the smugglers round these parts. We know he also had at least one ship trading legitimately with the West Indies and America. We can guess, now we know about the tunnel from his vault to the Dragon's Hole, that he must have had the tunnel improved and the tomb dug out at the end of it to provide a safe runway to the harbour and Pentarno haven, for a very practical purpose. What could be more respected than a family tomb? And what could make better cover for the secret road to the sea and the ships? He completed it about six years before he died. Maybe he always had in mind that it might eventually provide a way of retreat, if Cornwall ever got too hot to hold him.

" Well, now, suppose that the authorities and the preventives were closing in on this local hero, and finally had something on him that he wasn't going to be able to duck? I think there are signs that they would have welcomed an opportunity to bring him down. Most of the gentry dabbled in smuggling, but in a mild, personal way. Treverra went beyond that. Not for profit, probably, so much as for fun. He liked pulling their legs, and leading them by the nose. They wouldn't forgive him that. He resigned from the bench, where by all accounts he was a pretty generous and fair-minded Justice. I think he knew his scope here was narrowing. And then, you see, any of the local people who heard of any threat to him would warn him. He was the idol of the coast. Yes, I think he knew time was getting short, and made his plans accordingly. Among other things, he wrote his epitaph. And hers, I'm almost sure, was written at the same time, by her, by him, or by both together, I can't be sure. But I like to think of them sitting here, in this very room, with their heads together, capping each other's lines, and laughing over the supreme joke of their shared and audacious career. Look at Morwenna's face! That lovely, fragile creature was a lot more than a sleeping partner.

"So there's Treverra, only fifty-two years old, in the very prime of his life and vigour and powers, and the authorities closing in for the kill. And what happens?

"Treverra 'dies', and is buried. In the tomb he had made for himself, with the swivel-stone in the corner giving access to the cave and the harbour.

"And at night he arises, this 'dead' man, after all the decorous funeral business is over and the mourners have gone away. Maybe he was provided with a good crowbar inside the coffin for the occasion, even more probably he was also visited and helped out by his older son after dark. He had two sons. The elder was just twenty at this time, the younger was a schoolboy of fourteen. I think the elder was certainly in all the plans, you'll see why when we come to the case of Morwenna. Treverra, then, emerges from his tomb exceedingly alive and lusty, and retires gaily by his back way, from which, at low tide, he can reach either Maymouth harbour or Pentarno haven. What does it matter which he used? At either one or the other a boat is put in for him, to take him aboard ship—his own ship or another—and ship him away to the reserve fortune he's been salting away in readiness in the year-long summer of the West Indies.

"A sunshine cruise to an island paradise, just as Dominic said, if I'd only listened to him. But not Tir-nan-Og! Not even the Bahamas, perhaps, but near enough. According to the records most of his trading had been done with Trinidad, Tobago and Barbados. Somewhere there, I judge, we might still pick up his traces.

"How many were in the know? It's guesswork, now, but I'd say just the three of them, Jan, Morwenna and their elder son, and maybe the skipper of his ship. There may have been a family doctor in it, too, to cover the deaths, but if so, he kept his mouth tightly shut afterwards to protect himself, and who can blame him? They may have managed without him? It hardly matters now. I'm sure that's what happened. It accounts for the empty coffin, that was later to be filled and over-filled. And it accounts for what followed.

"For, you see, Morwenna would never have agreed to such a plan if there hadn't been provision in it for her to join him. Act two was to be the translation of Morwenna. She was to pine away—her own touch, that, I'd swear—and to be reunited with her lord in an earthly, not a heavenly, paradise. After six months the same programme is put in motion for her. She 'dies' of a broken heart, and is buried in the tomb prepared for her."

He broke off there, startled, for someone had uttered an almost inaudible sound that yet had the sharpness of a cry. A quiver passed round the circle, and a rustle of breath, as if they had all been shaken out of a trance. Paddy, flushing hotly, drew back a little into shadow. "I'm sorry! I was only thinking—She was so *little*!"

"They took every possible care of her, Paddy. Or they thought they had. Yes, she was very slight and frail, she couldn't deal with tombstones herself, they knew that. She had to lie patiently in her coffin until dark, when her son would come to release her, and see her safely down the passage and aboard. The light wooden coffin in which she was carried to the vault was pierced in a pattern of fine holes just above her face—did you notice that, George? The air in the stone coffin would easily be enough to keep her going until night. And she was well provided with funds for the journey, in money and jewellery. The wooden lid would be only very lightly fastened down, so that she could move it herself. And all she needed besides was the heart of a lioness, and that she knew she had. *She* was the one who misquoted Dryden, that I'd swear to. 'None but the brave deserves the brave.' To lie and wait several hours alone in the dark didn't seem terrible to her, not by comparison with what it bought.

"But that night of her funeral, you remember, is recorded as the night of the great storm, when the fishing-boats were driven out to sea. And young Treverra, the new squire, was blown from the cliff path in the darkness, and drowned. A young man in mourning, wandering the cliffs alone—no one would ask what he was doing there.

"I'm afraid, I'm terribly afraid, he was on his way down the cliff path to the church and the vault, to see his mother resurrected and put safely aboard ship for Barbados.

"And no one else, you see, knew anything about her.

"No one else. She was dead, they'd just buried her. *If* the doctor knew, he'd assume everything was going according to plan, or at least that her son was taking care of her, until he heard of the boy being missing. And that may not have happened until well into the next morning. By then a doctor would know she'd be dead. He'd be afraid to speak. It couldn't help her, and it could, you see, harm not only himself but Treverra, too. He'd be a wanted man again as soon as it was known he was alive. And nothing and nobody could give Morwenna back to him now."

"But the ship," ventured Dominic huskily. "There was a ship lying off for her. Wouldn't they try to find out what had happened?"

"That's what makes me think that this time it wasn't their own ship. It would be risky to chance having it stopped in these waters, obviously. No, this time I think it was a matter of a simple commercial arrangement with some other skipper, in which case they wouldn't know anything except that they were to put in a boat at such and such a spot and pick up a lady. If they ever did manage to put in a boat in such a sea, it's certain she didn't come to keep the appointment. They couldn't know what that implied, to them it just meant their passenger hadn't turned up. Maybe they waited as long as they could, maybe they were driven out. What could they do but sail without her?

"And all that money, and the valuables she was to have taken with her, just lay uselessly in her coffin with her for two centuries, until Zeb Trethuan found it and started methodically turning it into money again. Thus setting the stage for the next death.

"Nobody knew about it, you see. Young Treverra's body was never found, so the vault wasn't opened for him. His young brother came home from school and took over the estate, but he'd never been in the secret. To him his mother and father had died and been buried, no mysteries, no tragedy but the ordinary, gentle tragedy of bereavement, that happens sooner or later to everyone. By the time *he* died and was buried, St. Nectan's was already fighting a losing battle with the sand, and they'd built St. Mary's, high up in the town, and abandoned the old graveyard by the shore. And Morwenna lay there alone, separated from her Jan, and he—God knows which was the unluckier of the two."

Tamsin had got up from her place very quietly, and gone to her desk. She came back with the folder of the Treverra papers in her hand, and slid out upon the table the two epitaphs.

"Not that I don't know them by heart," she said in a low voice. "But suddenly they seem so new and so transparent, as though we ought to have been able to read the whole story in them from the beginning."

"You think I've made out a case, then?" Simon's eyes met hers down the length of the table, and there was nothing left of challenge or antagonism on her side, and nothing of pursuit or self-indulgence on his. They looked at each other with wonder and grief, and a certain frustrated help-lessness, but with no doubt at all.

" I think it's so unanswerable a case that I don't know how we missed following the clues Jan left us. It's all *here*! Don't you hear him? He couldn't play any game without making it dangerous to himself, there wouldn't have been any sport. He told them just what he was about. He made his exit snapping his fingers under the nose of the law, and daring them to follow his trail if they had the wit. But they hadn't, and neither had we.

> ' *Think not to find, beneath this Stone,*
> *Mute Witness, bleached, ambiguous Bone*———'

You see, he told them, don't look for me here, you won't find me. And then, his ' trackless maze,' ' the labyrinth beyond the tomb '—what was that but the real tunnel that opened beyond *his* tomb? He told them how he made his getaway, kicked up his heels at them and invited them to go after him if they were smart enough. And then, the last four lines, those are for *her*.

> ' *There follow, O my Soul, and find*
> *Thy Lord as ever true and kind,*
> *And savour, where all Travellers meet,*
> *The last Love as the first Love sweet* '."

Simon sat looking at her with a face very still and very pale beneath its tan, and eyes that had no lustre; his voice was gentle and impersonal enough as he took up the recital from her.

" Now listen to Morwenna, and I don't think you'll doubt that this really was Morwenna herself speaking :

> ' *Carve this upon Morwenna's Grave:*
> NONE BUT THE BRAVE DESERVES THE BRAVE.
> *Shed here no Tears. No Saint could die*
> *More blessed and comforted than I.*

For I confide I shall but rest
A Moment in this stony Nest,
Then, raised by Love, go forth to find
A Country dearer to my Mind,
And touching safe the sun-bright Shore,
Embrace my risen Lord once more.'

Well, do you hear the authentic voice?"

They heard it indeed, suddenly fierce, impious, arrogant and gay, the reverse of its own conventionally presented image. Miss Rachel stirred uneasily, unwilling to acknowledge but unable to deny what she now saw in that delicate and beautiful creature in the drawing on the wall. Not the first and not the last in history to spit unwise defiance at the lightning.

"Why, she was the wilder of the two! That's surely more than a little blasphemous! And then such a terrible fate, poor girl. Mr. Polwhele, do you think that what happened to them was a kind of *Judgment*?"

"No!" said the Vicar, with large and unclerical disdain, and looked a little surprised at his own vehemence. "I should be ashamed to attribute to God a malice of which I don't find even myself capable. And I don't think the spectacle of two daring and exuberant children egging each other on to say outrageous things about me, in my hearing, would even drive me to knock their heads together, much less drop a mountain on them and crush them. I think I might even laugh, when they weren't looking. It would depend on the degree of style they showed. And Morwenna certainly had style. No, I don't think there was any rejoicing in heaven when there was nobody left to lift the stone away. Rather a terrible sense of loss. She was brave, loyal and loving, enough virtues to offset what the Authorised Version would call a froward tongue. No, I suppose one must say that they played with fire so persistently that it was inevitable they'd get burned in the end. But to them playing with fire made life doubly worth living. You can't have it both ways."

"If she was blasphemous," said Phil, shivering, "she certainly paid for it. She had the more terrible fate."

"Did she?" Simon looked up, looked round the table with a brief and contorted smile. "I wonder how long Treverra watched and waited for her, or for news of her? He couldn't come home, you see, he couldn't even send letters, there was no one left here who knew he was alive. He had to stay dead in his old identity, he was still a wanted man. Maybe he thought she'd changed her mind, and found it quite convenient to be a widow. Maybe he thought she'd married again. Maybe he even began to fear she'd been planning her own future and laughing at him even while she helped him to arrange his elaborate joke, She was only forty-one, and a great beauty. And he couldn't come back and fight for her. His joke had turned against him. Oh, believe me, if there was anything he had to pay for, he paid. There was only one agony he was spared— at least he didn't know how his darling died."

: :   : :

The moon was up when they went out to the cars, not too late, because Paddy had to leave by the traditional mid-morning train, and there were still the last little things to pack. The tide was half-way out, the moonshine turned the wet beach to silver, and the scattered clouds were moist with reflected light.

"I trust," said Simon, finding George Felse close beside him as they went down the steps to the drive, "you were duly impressed with my performance?"

The voice was deliberately cool and light, but tired. He had walked rather stiffly past Tamsin, when she hesitated and waited for him in the doorway. For several days now he had been walking past Tamsin, with aching care and reluctant resolution. It had taken her a day or so to realise it, and longer to believe in it. She had the idea now, she had betaken herself promptly where she was welcomed, between Paddy and Dominic. They stood chattering beside the Mini, all a little subdued. The soft voices had a sound of autumn in them, too, as gentle as the salt wind.

"Yes, you're quite a detective," conceded George. Simon's eyes were on Paddy, and the slight, brooding smile was unwary; he had no reason to suppose that George possessed the knowledge necessary to make it significant. "Now what about tackling the only mystery that's left? I'm sure you could put a finger just as accurately on Trethuan's killer, if you really tried."

The smile stiffened slightly for an instant, and then perceptibly deepened. "Maybe I will, yet," said Simon. "But there's just one more question I have to ask before I shall know what I've got to tell you about that case. Give me till to-morrow."

"I'll do that."

"Can I run you back to the hotel? It isn't too comfortable for four, but it's bearable for that distance."

"Thanks, but we'll walk. It's not far, and rather nice at this time of night. And I think we'll make our farewells to Paddy now. To-morrow," said George quite gently, "had better be left to the family. Don't you think so?"

::   ::

The question that was to determine the ending of the Trethuan case was asked later that same night. And the person who had to answer it was Paddy Rossall.

They were all together round the fire before bed, Paddy's packing done, the last pot of tea circulating, when Simon said in a careful and unemphatic voice, so that the shock came only gradually, like the late breaking of a wave:

"I hadn't intended to do this, and if the truth hadn't come out without any act of mine, I never would. But now we all know where we are. Paddy, you're fifteen, for all present purposes you're a man. You know I'm your father, as well as I know it. Now I want to talk to you, here, now, with Tim and Phil present, the only honest way."

The silence that fell was extreme. There might never have been sound or movement in the world.

"Simon," began Tim quietly, when he had his voice again, "do you think this is fair?"

"Yes, I think it's fair. I think it's absolutely necessary.

We've been stalling it since yesterday morning, since we all knew where we stood. It's necessary for us all, if only to clear the air. I am who I am, and Paddy knows it now, why not say it? Paddy, you *do* know. Say it!"

" Simon, you've no right——"

Phil laid her hand restrainingly on her husband's arm. He had expected her to blaze into indignation, and she was silent; it confused and calmed him at the same time, effectively silencing him.

"Yes, I know," said Paddy in a small, tight voice. He had a cup of tea in his hand; he laid it down carefully on the tiled hearth, and wiped his palms slowly on his thighs. His face was taut and expressionless.

"Then listen to me. This once listen to me, and be sure I respect you and trust you to be honest. We all want you to be happy, to have a full life and a satisfying life. I'm going to speak up for myself now. It's the first time I've been able to do that, and I don't see why I shouldn't take advantage of it. I know I'm very late in making my bid, Paddy, but I've got a lot to offer. I've got an assignment that's going to take me practically round the world for a series of articles and broadcasts. If you choose, you can come with me. It's entirely up to you. Everything I can give you, I'll give. Everything I can do for you, I'll do. I want you, Paddy, I want you very much. I'll do everything possible to try and deserve you, if you'll come with me."

" Now, look !" growled Tim.

" No, Tim, let him talk." Phil drew him down again to his chair and held him there, charmed into quiescence by her bewildering serenity. It was too late, in any case, to deflect the encounter. The matter had been taken out of their hands, but for all that it was not yet in Simon's. Paddy was a person, too. They must place as much reliance in him as Simon did, they had better reason. Nobody must argue back. Their arguments were already on record, fifteen years of them, without any world-tours, without any glamour, inexpert, imperfect, intimate arguments. But

Phil knew their weight, and had already bet her life and Tim's on their validity.

So Simon was the only one who talked; and Simon was an unmatched talker when his heart was in it. He was ruthless, too, now that he was in pursuit of something he really wanted. Miss Rachel had been a shrewd prophet.

"That's all, Paddy. You know what you've got here, and now you know what I'm promising you. It's up to you. If you decide to come with me, I don't believe Tim and Phil will stand in your way." It was a fighting case he'd made, he felt drained with all that had gone out of him. And Paddy sat there with his hands clenched on his thighs, and his face white with tension, staring into the fire.

"Paddy, look at me!"

Paddy raised his head obediently, and met Simon's eyes full. His mouth and chin were set like stone, as if he felt the threat of tears not far away.

"Will you come?"

Paddy's lips parted slowly and painfully. He moistened them, and tried for a voice that creaked and failed him; tried again, and achieved a remarkably steady, loud and controlled utterance.

"I'm sorry, but this is where I belong. With my parents. I like you very much, and of course you're my father's best friend. But I'm not going anywhere, except back to school to-morrow. But thank you," he ended with punctilious politeness, "for asking me."

He uncurled his closed fingers with a wrench, and got to his feet abruptly, all his movements slightly stiff and careful.

"If you'll excuse me, I'll go to bed now. Good-night, Mummy!" The quick, current touch of his lips on her cheek forbade her to manifest either surprise or concern. "Good-night, Dad!" His hand patted Tim's shoulder lightly in passing. He was half-way to the door, magnificent and precarious, passing close to where Simon stood stricken mute and rigid with shock. And then he spoiled the whole gallant show.

It was not a deliberate blow; he had hesitated and cast

about him frantically for a second to find some formula he could use, but there was none, and the instant of silence grew enormous in his own ears, and had to be broken. You can't just excise a human being from your life, and pretend he doesn't exist, you can't call him " Uncle Simon " when he's just reminded you that he isn't anything of the kind, you can't say " Father " when you have a father already, and have just been at pains to point out that you have no intention whatever of swopping him for anybody else on earth. There wasn't anything left but that in-alienable possession, a name, and only the respectful form was even half-way appropriate.

He said : " Good-night, Mr. Towne !", fighting off the silence in sheer panic, and instantly and horribly aware that even the silence had been preferable.

Simon jerked back his head and drew in breath pain-fully, as if he had been struck in the face. He reached out a hand in incredulous protest, and caught the boy by the arm.

" My dear *child*——!"

Paddy turned upon him a pale face suddenly and briefly convulsed by a bright blaze of anger and desperation, and struck as hard as he could, frantic to end this and escape.

" That's just the point ! I'm not a child any longer, I'm not all that dear to you, and above all, I'm *not yours*. You gave me away, remember?"

For one electrifying instant Phil saw the two fierce, strained faces braced close to each other, staring in mutual anguish, more alike than they had ever been before. Then Paddy tugged his arm free and stalked out of the room; but in a moment they heard him climbing the stairs at a wild run, head-down for the privacy of his own room.

Simon hung still for a long, incredulous moment, his hand still extended, unable to grasp what had happened to him. Its finality there was no mistaking, but it took him what seemed an age to comprehend and accept it. He turned from them in a blind man's walk, and went and groped out a cigarette from the box on the table, to find his shaking hands something challenging and normal to do.

Phil had risen instinctively and taken a couple of hasty steps towards the door to follow Paddy, but then she checked after all, and sat down again slowly. She felt for Tim's hand, and closed her fingers on it gratefully. Simon's fair crest, pale against the dark curtains, Simon's rigid shoulders and patient, obstinate hands at work with matches, seemed to her suddenly close kin to Paddy's beloved person, and infinitely more in need of pity.

"I ought to take you apart," said Tim roused and scowling.

"Think you could do a better job than Paddy just did?" asked the taut voice.

"You asked for it."

"I know I did. And I got it. Between the eyes." He was ready to turn and face them now, the faintest of smiles wry at the corners of his mouth. "Don't worry! I know when I'm licked. Even if I never had much practice, I can still be a sporting loser when there's no help for it. I apologise, Tim, it was a dirty trick. It won't happen again. Ever."

"I tried to warn you," said Phil in a very low voice.

"I know you did. I ought to have remembered that most women never bet anything that really matters to them, except on certainties. I won't forget again."

"Simon," she said impulsively, gripping Tim's hand tightly, because of course Tim didn't understand, and probably never would, "settle for what you can get. There *is* something that belongs to you. I know it isn't what you wanted, but it's too good to throw away."

Simon came across the room to her, took her chin in his hand, and kissed her. "God bless you, Phil! I'll take any crumb that's offered. But I don't deserve a damn' thing, and I won't ask for anything again. After to-morrow, I promise, you won't be bothered with me any more."

CHAPTER XI

MONDAY MORNING

PADDY CAME DOWN next morning pale and quiet, but resolutely calm, and very much in command of himself and circumstances. There were the blessed, beastly, ordinary details of returning to school to be taken care of, and no drama at all, and no opportunity for introspection. He had worked out his own course overnight, even before his mother had looked in almost guiltily to kiss him good-night all over again, and found him composed and ready for sleep. He had been glad to be visited, all the same; it's fine not to need comfort, but it's nice to know that it's ready and waiting if you should want it.

"I hope I wasn't rude, Mummy. I didn't mean to be. I was a bit pushed, not having any warning."

"I know. Don't worry, you weren't rude."

She tucked him in, a piece of pure self-indulgence, for Paddy had never looked so adult and self-sufficient as he did now. He smiled up at her with understanding and affection, but very gravely.

"Mummy—will *he* be all right?"

"He'll be all right. We'll see that he is."

She was quick to know what he wanted. It was she who made a point of inviting Simon to drive in with them to the station, and so gave Paddy himself the opportunity of seconding the invitation.

"Yes, do come. Of course there's plenty of room. My trunk's gone on ahead, there's only a small case to take."

So there were four of them in the Mini on the way to the station, Simon in the front seat beside Tim, the pair of them taciturn as yet; Paddy and his mother in the back, cosy and a little disconsolate together. There's something at once damping and heartening about the beginning of a new term.

"It was a lovely holiday, darling, I'm sorry it's over. Don't forget to write every week-end. There'll be ructions if you don't."

"I'll be chivvied into it, don't worry. But I wouldn't forget, anyhow. Cheer up, it won't be long till Christmas." It seemed an age away, but he knew from experience how soon it would be sitting on the doorstep. He nuzzled Phil's shoulder briefly and happily; and presently a corner of his mind defected flightily to consider the Middle School's football prospects for the new season, even before he had taken care of all his responsibilities here at home.

They disembarked beside the blonde wooden fence of the station approach, and unloaded the suitcase with due ceremony, already worrying vainly about whether anything had been forgotten.

"I'll say good-bye here," said Simon, with the right lightness of tone, if not of heart. "I've got a call I want to make in the town. So long, Paddy, have a good journey. And a good term!"

"Thanks very much!" He had saved it until then, to give it its maximum effect. He gripped Simon's hand with warmth, but still with some reserve. "Good-bye,——" His face flamed, but the blue eyes never wavered. "—*Uncle Simon*!"

: :   : :

Simon turned away briskly, and walked the length of the light-brown barrier with an even pace and a jaunty bearing, balancing with care the great, hollow ache of Paddy's charity within him; and alongside the extreme end of the platform a lean quiet man was propped against the fence with arms folded, watching the lower school starlings gather and shrill greetings, and the self-conscious young cock-pheasants of the sixth stroll from their parents' sides to knot themselves into world-weary conversations with their own kind. They had about as much control over their sophistication as over their feet, and their graces were as endearing as one's first-born's fledgling efforts on the amateur stage. The in-betweens, like Paddy, had the best of both worlds, rollercoasting without pretence from lofty dignity to uninhibited horse-play, and back again. They could even stand and wait, as Paddy did, warmly linked with their parents, and openly happy to have them close for a few more minutes; for they had outgrown homesickness, and quite forgotten the ancient dread of tears, but had not yet grown into that extreme state of senior self-consciousness which scorns to have had a human origin at all, and prefers not to have its parents around for fear they shall somehow fall short of the ideal image.

"On the whole," said George Felse, turning from the spectacle with the small, private smile still on his lips, "I must say they inspire me with a degree of self-satisfaction. Wouldn't it be simpler, though, to put boy and trunk and paraphernalia into the Land-Rover, and just drive them the twelve miles there, and tip 'em out?"

"They wouldn't consider it for a moment. This always has been the school train, and it always will be. It's better for the little ones," said Simon. "By the time they get there the ice is well and truly broken, and they've been doused a couple of times, and got over the cold and the shock, even begun to enjoy it. Twelve miles is just long enough."

"I see," said George, falling into step beside him, "you've got the basic knowledge necessary to a father."

"But not the other basic requirements. Cigarette?" They halted for a moment over the lighted match, faces close, and again fell into step together. Simon drew in smoke hungrily, and let it go in a long, soundless sigh. "Yes —I promised you a solution, didn't I?"

"You promised, at least, to let me know whether you could provide one or not. When you'd asked your final question."

"I've asked it. And it's been answered." He walked for a minute in silence, his eyes on the ground. "Not that I really have anything to tell you. You already know—don't you?"

"I've known all along," said George, "who put him there. I didn't know who'd killed him until Miss Rachel mentioned that you were sitting on the lawn talking to her about Paddy, the afternoon *he* was there in the garden, picking plums. Only a few hours before he died. And even now," he said with intent, " I couldn't prove it."

" I shouldn't worry," said Simon. " You don't have to prove it. Paddy turned me down."

Silence for a moment. They walked together equably, down the cobbled paving of a narrow street leading towards the town. Behind them, in the heathy fringes of the uplands, a train whistle sounded.

" If Paddy had opted for me—but I see I was mad ever to think he might—I'd have kept my mouth tight shut and ridden it out, and let you prove it if you could. I'd have taken him and got out. But he turned me down. Flatter than I've ever been turned down in my life, and harder. And now, do you know, on the whole I find myself preferring it this way. My instincts are incurably on the side of justice, after all." He dug his hands deep into his pockets, hunching his shoulders against the sudden cold wind from the sea. " I gathered last night that you knew already Paddy was—or rather used to be—mine."

" I happened to be with Phil, the night we were hunting for him, when Miss Rachel finally admitted what she'd done. Phil said in any case she couldn't have told him *who* his father was, because she didn't know it. And the old lady said oh, yes, she did, she'd learned it from you yourself, no longer ago than Wednesday afternoon, sitting in the garden. Don't worry, I haven't told anyone else. I never shall."

" And how did you know the rest of it? What was it that told you?"

" A number of small things. First, that you asked me to be there at all. I'd been with you most of one evening and part of the next morning, and you hadn't found it necessary to draft me in. But five minutes after Paddy had let it out that I was C.I.D. by profession, you asked me to make one in your team. I knew there had to be a reason. You hardly knew me as a person, you'd invited me as what you did now know me to be, a policeman, but a policeman on holiday, out of his own manor, without any local connections or loyalties. I couldn't imagine why you wanted such a person, and why you wanted him suddenly on the last day. Not until we were confronted with a body. Then I knew. You wanted an accurate and unbiased observer. You wanted no one involved because of haphazard evidence. You wanted to be fair to all those who might otherwise come under suspicion. So you'd known he was going to be found there. So you'd put him there. It was as simple as that. Everything else had to fit in. And the whole organisation of that affair, the whole set-up in the vault, did fit in. The discovery had been staged. And there was only one possible stage-manager. And other, personal things, fitted in, too. You began to avoid Tamsin. Forgive me if I'm trampling rather crudely through things you'd prefer to keep well apart from this. But you asked me how I knew. You've kept carefully away from her for the last five days. But not—forgive me again!—not because you stopped wanting her. And then, when Paddy went missing, you were the one who said he'd turn up safe and sound. Knowing, of course, that he had nothing at all to fear from our supposed murderer-at-large. It was only later, when time wore on and he still didn't show up, that you got really frightened about him. Do you want me to go on?"

Simon broke step to tread out his cigarette at the edge of the pavement. The incredible hydrangeas of Cornwall foamed over a garden wall and filled his eyes with blue and rose and violet.

"Yes, go on. I'm interested."

"Every soul in this district knew the tomb was going to be opened, and nobody knew it better than you. So when you put the dead man there, or at least when you elected to leave him there, it was because you *wanted him found*. Well, that didn't surprise me very much. Supposing you were responsible for his death in some way, you might well prefer it like that, if you could arrange it in circumstances that wouldn't point straight at you. You'd want, other things being equal, to be fair to his family, not to leave them on thorns, not knowing whether he was alive or dead. But if you wanted him found, and if, as seemed likely, he'd drowned in the sea and been washed up on the Mortuary, then why not just leave him to be found there? And there was an answer to that, too. All the time we've been staying here, the first bather on that beach every morning has been young Paddy.

"And you wouldn't want Paddy to be the one to find him. Not even just because of the ugliness. This man had died, in a way, because of Paddy, and you couldn't bear that there should be any closer link than existed already in your mind. It was shock enough when you heard he'd glimpsed him in the sea, the evening before, wasn't it? And then, you'd promised Paddy to tell the coastguard, and I know you didn't, even after Dominic mentioned it in the bar at night, and reminded you. You didn't forget. You don't forget promises to Paddy.

"But there wasn't a ghost of a motive. Not even when it came out that Trethuan had been trying to threaten or persuade you into leaving the vault alone. What did you care for his threats? He had no hold on you. No, what I was inclined to think, up to then, was that you knew who *had* killed him, and were covering up for the guilty party because you didn't think of him as a murderer, but at the same time trying to protect the innocent from suspicion. And then Miss Rachel let it out that he'd been there in the kitchen garden of Treverra Place, just at the time when you were there with her on the lawn, telling her that Paddy is your son. Trethuan had followed you down from the churchyard, after you brushed him off for the last time. He was desperate to stop you, by any means. Whether he would have tried to put *you* out of the way, too, if everything else had failed, one can't be sure. But it's worth considering, isn't it?"

He flashed a glance along his shoulder, and saw Simon's clear profile beside him, fixed as bronze, the lines of jaw and cheekbone pale with tension. "I suppose he might have tried it. I hadn't thought. He didn't, though."

"No, what happened wasn't in self-defence, I realise

that. All the same, he was dogging your steps, in search of anything, any mortal thing, that could be used to bring you to heel or shut you up for good. And he was in the kitchen garden. Picking plums, maybe, but only because where the plums were he could listen to your conversation, and be ready to continue his pursuit of you.

"I don't suppose he heard everything. What he did hear meant just one thing to him, didn't it? Just one obvious, crude but possibly useful thing.

"And then you left the Place, and went out along the Dragon's Head, alone, at an hour when it was deserted. Having a lot of not very happy thinking to do, and plenty of time before you were expected home to tea. And Trethuan made his excuse to Miss Rachel in a great hurry, promised to finish the job next day, and made off after you. He thought he had what he needed, now. He thought he could make you dance to his tune. He came to you, I judge, somewhere near the point, up on the cliff path. He'd want a solitary place. I can guess what he said.

"Yes—he had a simple sort of mind. Not nice, but simple. It wasn't Paddy *he* threatened to tell—was it?"

They had come down to the southern corner of the harbour, and halted there to lean on the railings shoulder to shoulder, looking out over the smooth brown mud and the stranded boats close to them, and the gleaming quiet water beyond, lipping so softly now at the masonry of the mole. Watery sun gilded the small, scalloped waves. The tide was well out, but not yet at its lowest. Simon clenched his hands on the rail, and stared blindly before him, and the screaming flight of gulls wheeling round them was only a pattern of sound to him for a moment. He shut his eyes hard, and shook his head, and the dizziness passed.

"I'm sorry!" he said. "I haven't been sleeping so well." He passed a hand over his eyes, and in a moment he said: "No, it wasn't Paddy!" and again was silent.

"You'd better tell it," George said reasonably. "You know best."

"You know already. It was just as you said. It was the

blind, bloody meanness and stupidity of it that got me,"
he said, suddenly shivering with detestation. "I blow up,
sometimes. One thing Paddy's got from me, worse luck!
—wouldn't you know it would be something like that I'd
give him?—is that temper of his. If you've ever seen
it in action? No, I suppose not. Tim's the patient one,
Tim's done wonders with him. But it can still happen,
to Paddy and to me. And there was this creature capering
and crowing that he'd heard me admit Paddy was my son!
You're so right, to him that meant just one thing, and he
thought it was all he needed. If I wouldn't call the whole
thing off, *he'd tell Tim*!

"It was ludicrous, it didn't mean a thing, it was no threat
to anyone, how could it be? I burst out laughing in his
face. And then he called Phil—the sort of name—*Phil*!
The truest soul alive, and the one I've injured most already!

"And *I hit him*.

"I don't know if it makes sense to you. It was somehow the one thing I couldn't stand. After all I'd done
to them, making use of them for my own ends when it
suited me, and then wanting to steal Paddy back—because
I did want to, very badly. And then on top of everything,
this futile, meaningless, humiliating bit of dirt. You can't
imagine how horribly it offended."

"I think," said George mildly, "I can. You're sure
he didn't lose his head and hit out at you first? Or shape
towards it? When you laughed at him, for instance?"

"Don't tempt me, George. I'm a dodger but not a liar.
He never raised a hand."

"Did you ever, even for an instant, mean to kill him?"

"Good lord, no! Well,—I don't think so. I don't know
that I *meant* anything. I just blew up. I hit him with
everything I'd got, but I give you my word I only hit
him once. I even woke up in time to make one wild grab
at him as he dropped, but he slipped through my fingers.
I'd turned, you see, when he came up to me, there was
the rise of the Dragon's Head on my right, and the drop
to the deep water outside the haven on my left. If I lash
out, it's always with the right. I hadn't thought how it

would swing him round. I hadn't thought at all, it was too quick for thought. It wasn't quite a sheer fall, we weren't that near the edge. He went lurching two or three strides downward, and then lost his footing and rolled. Before I could slither after him he was over the edge. He dropped into the deep water. I think he must have been stunned, because he never came up."

The lines of strain had eased a little, blood was coming back to his face. He drew breath deeply, and let go of the rail.

"We'd better be moving along, hadn't we?"

"When you're ready."

"You're not in any hurry to turn me in, are you?" said Simon, with the first reviving smile.

"I'm not turning you in. And there never was any hurry. We hadn't got a murderer at large to worry about. Go on, if you care to. You went in after him, didn't you?"

"How did you know that?" He was capable of feeling surprise again.

"Because you went in again with Dominic afterwards, so long afterwards that it couldn't have been with any hope of finding him alive. It must have been full tide when he fell, if there was deep water off the haven. It was at least half an hour past when you showed up on the beach with the boys. So either it was just for the look of the thing generally—which isn't entirely convincing where you're concerned—or because you wanted to account satisfactorily for wet hair and wet underclothes. The boys wouldn't be noticing that you were wet already, before you went in, they were much too preoccupied then."

"That's pretty good, but I can tell you one more reason. I'd skinned my knuckles on the right hand, when I hit him. Diving and swimming round those rocks, I made the other hand match. I hadn't thought about that the first time. You can get cut about quite extensively if you're not careful. Paddy was quite concerned, when we were cleaning up afterwards, and he saw them." He looked down with a dark, remembering smile at the backs of his hands, the points of the knuckles still marked with small, healed lesions.

"Yes, I went in after him. I scrambled down the rock path, and shed my top clothes, and dived and dived for him until I was worn out, and by then it would have been no good, anyhow. It was pretty rough going, but I'm a strong swimmer. And after that, I suppose, it came over me what I'd done, and I knew I had to get away from there, fast. I couldn't get through the Dragon's Hole, or I'd have beat it through there and let myself be seen along the harbour. But it was deep under water at that time. All I could do was put on my clothes and bolt back up the cliff path, and work round by the Maymouth side on to the road. And when I came up over the neck on my way home I saw your boy hauling Paddy out of the rough water. I ran down to them, and you know the rest. I went in and worked hard for the complete answer to why my hair was wet and my knuckles skinned. Praying we wouldn't find him. Praying he'd never be found.

"And that's all. Except that Sam said, that night, he'd probably come in on the Mortuary with the next high tide. That gave me a shock. I'm not a native, that was something I didn't know."

"And the first thing you thought of was Paddy running down to the beach about seven o'clock in the morning and finding him."

"Wouldn't it be the first thing that would have occurred to you? If the body was going to be cast up here, I wanted to be the one to find it, not Paddy. I was awake all night, brooding about it, and before it was light I got up and dressed, and sneaked out while everybody else was asleep. High tide was about a quarter past four that morning. I bet I was down on the shore before five.

"And he was there! I hadn't really believed in it till then, but he was there. Miles of sand every way, and he was a big fellow, and dead weight. And the sea was no good, the sea wouldn't have him. There was only the church anywhere near for a hiding-place. And the key of the vault was in my pocket. So I put him in there. We had crowbars and wedges down there, already, waiting for the big job. I suppose I thought I could move him again the next night. Maybe I didn't think at all, just huddled him out of sight. It was getting light, and all the time I had Paddy on my mind. It was quite a job, single-handed, but it can be done if you're pushed."

"So you very honestly explained to me," said George, "when I asked you, yesterday."

"Well, by instinct I am honest. I've never had any reason to be anything else, before. It gets everything snarled up, though, when you do get into a jam. Well, I got him into the coffin. I thought I was putting him in with Treverra. And all the time I was shutting him in with the man he'd killed two years before. Who says providence hasn't got a sense of humour?

"And yet it doesn't make me feel a bit better about it, that he turned out to be a murderer. It doesn't alter anything.

"And then afterwards, when I began thinking where I'd move him to, I thought, well, why? Why move him at all? For all I knew then, he had a loving family. I don't think I'd ever wanted to deprive them of him, and I didn't really like the thought of them waiting and worrying, and looking for him, not even knowing whether he was alive or dead. *Never* knowing. I'd killed him, and that was bad enough. But I found my conscience was going to give me double hell if I tried to sneak out and leave them to fret, and justice to fumble around without any hold on me. But most of all, I suspect, I simply hated and dreaded the thought of touching him again, and going on with this awful game of hide-and-seek. Oh, I wanted to get off scot-free, if I could. Half of me did, anyhow. But not quite on those terms. So I thought, all right, let it just happen. We're going to open the tomb, right, we'll open it. Murder will out, let it at least out in a decent, orderly fashion, with no kids and no women to happen on it unawares, and nobody to give emotional and misleading evidence that can land some innocent person in trouble. That's why I asked you to make one."

They had walked the length of one little shopping street from the end of the harbour, and emerged into the square.

Without consultation, but quite naturally, they crossed the cobbled space of parked cars towards the door of the police station.

"I'm glad I did," said Simon, producing suddenly, even out of his profound depression, the smile that drew people after him.

"You didn't need me," said George. "This has been your show throughout."

They reached the apron of paving before the steps, and halted there by consent to take breath before entering Neither of them noticed the light flurry of steps on the cobbles, heading for them at a confident run from the newsagent's shop at the corner of the square.

"Well, that was exactly how it happened. Pointless and needless. Nobody even wanted it. But it happened, and I was the one who made it happen." Simon filled his lungs deeply, as though there was going to be less to breathe inside. Very soberly he asked: "What do you think I shall get?"

The running feet broke rhythm, suddenly and very close to them. A breath caught on a half-sound, as if someone had been about to speak quite loudly and gaily, and then swallowed the word unspoken. George swung round, and found himself staring into the wide, wary, golden-hazel eyes of his son.

"Dad, I—I was only——" His voice wavered away into uncertainty and silence. He looked from one face to the other with that bright, uneasy, intelligent glance, and drew back a step. "I'm sorry, I didn't mean to butt in. I'll see you later. It wasn't anything."

"That's all right, Dom," said George calmly. "But not now, we're occupied. Run off and take care of your mother, I'll be with you at lunch."

"Yes, of course. I didn't realise you were busy. Sorry!"

He drew back at once, gladly, quickly, but the stunned look in his eyes had begun to change before he turned his back on them and walked away rapidly out of the square, and the imagination behind the eyes was at work frantically with what he must certainly have heard. "It happened, and I was the one who made it happen. What do you think I shall get?" His innocent approach couldn't have been better timed to tell him everything in two sentences. And he was exceedingly quick in the uptake.

"I'm sorry about that," said Simon with compunction, looking after the slender figure as it walked too steadily, too thoughtfully, away from them. "But he'd have had to know pretty soon, I suppose. What *do* you think I shall get?"

"With luck," said George, "a discharge. At the worst, up to three years for manslaughter. If you tell it as you've told it to me."

"Ah, but I shan't be doing that. And neither will you, George, not quite. If they reduce the charge to manslaughter, or unlawful killing, or anything less than murder, I'm going to plead guilty. Then they won't have to call evidence at all—will they? So everyone will be spared."

"You'll do nothing of the sort," said George with equal firmness. "You'll employ a good lawyer, and be guided by him how to plead. You just tell the truth and leave the law to him. With any luck he'll get you off."

Simon's tawny face had recovered something of its spirit and audacity, and all of its obstinacy. "I'll tell the truth, and nothing but the truth, but not quite the whole truth. I'll say he came following and threatening me, I'll say he was abusive. And with what's going to come out about Ruiz, that won't be at all hard for them to believe and understand. But I won't bring Paddy and Tim and Phil into it. They're back safely on the rails, and running like a train, and I'm not going to do anything to shake them again, and neither are you. I'd rather plead guilty ten times over. I'm not what I'd call a good man, George, but that's one thing I won't do, and won't let you do, either. And unless you promise me here and now to keep them out of it, it's your word against mine for all this. I won't co-operate. I'll turn back here and deny everything, and make you sweat your case up as best you can. I don't believe you could ever make it stick."

"You wouldn't be happy," said George, smiling.

"No, I wouldn't. I'd much rather go in there and get it off my chest. But not at that price."

"I told you," said George, "*I'm* not turning you in. You brought yourself here. It's your show."

"Good, then they're out of it. For keeps. I look upon that as a promise, George. But—would you mind coming in with me? And will you be kind enough to let Tim know, afterwards? Don't let them worry. They'll know best how to tell Paddy. It isn't that I wanted to keep him from knowing," he said, as they climbed the steps side by side. "I just wanted him safely off the scene until I'd got the worst over."

The shadow of the doorway fell on him, softening the tight, bright lines of his face, braced again now for the ordeal.

"Oh, well," he said, with a small, hollow laugh, "I've never been in gaol before. It should be a rest-cure."

::   ::

From the corner of an alley at the far end of the square, Dominic watched them disappear into the dark doorway. When they were gone he came out of hiding, and began furiously to climb the steep streets inland, towards the upper town and Treverra Place. Inside him a weakening sceptic was still clamouring that it was impossible, that he was making a fool of himself, that there were dozens of possible interpretations of what he had heard, besides the obvious and yet obviously inaccurate one. But he went on walking, at his longest climbing stride, and with lungs pumping.

"Nobody even wanted it. But it happened, and I was the one who made it happen." And then, in that quiet voice: "What do you think I shall get?"

It had to mean what he thought it meant, there was nothing else it could mean. But in that case it could tell him more, if he looked closely enough and carefully enough. "Nobody even wanted it." It wasn't intended, it wasn't done deliberately. Not murder, then. "But it happened, and I was the one——" Still not murder, something that happened by Simon's act, possibly by Simon's fault, but not deliberately. Manslaughter, culpable homicide, but *not* murder. And he wasn't expecting extremes in the penalty, either. "What do you think I shall get?" Dominic wished he'd been clever enough to blunder in just two or three seconds later, in time to hear the reply. To make it easier to tell, to answer some of the frantic anxieties that would result, before they could even be voiced. Because there was still just one thing a knowledgeable friend could do for Simon, in this extremity. And Dominic was the one person who knew exactly how to do it.

He arrived blown and panting at the absurd, top-heavy gates of Treverra Place, and took the drive a little more soberly, to recover his breath.

Tamsin was in the library, copy-typing catalogue notes, her underlip caught between her teeth, the reddish-gold fringe on her forehead bouncing gently to the slight vibration of her head. He marched straight to her desk, leaned a hand on either side the typewriter, and looked down into the startled face that warmed immediately into a smile for him. He wondered why he felt like the bearer of good news, when he was only the messenger of disaster. Still, you may as well pick up the better pieces even of a catastrophe, and see what they'll make when you put them together.

"Tamsin, I've got something very urgent to tell you. I just ran slam into Dad and Simon outside the police station, and from what I heard, Simon has just given himself up for killing Trethuan." That's the way news should be delivered, if you want to know what people really feel about it.

"*Simon?*" cried Tamsin, eyes and tone flaring into partisan anger and derision. She was on her feet. "Simon *murder* someone? You're out of your mind."

"I didn't say murder, I said killing. They were perfectly calm but deadly serious. And they've gone into the police station. I'd say what's in the wind is manslaughter, at most. But it *was* Simon, I heard him say it himself. He said: 'Nobody even wanted it. But it happened, and I was the one who made it happen.' And then he asked Dad: 'What do you think I shall get?' Now you know everything I know. And what," demanded Dominic, jutting his jaw at her, "are you going to do about it?"

She was a remarkable girl, he'd always known it. She had exclaimed once, and there was no more of that. She caught him by the shoulders and held him before her, so hard that she left the marks of her fingers on his arms, while she searched his face with wild blue eyes that had been like cornflowers a moment ago, and were now like spears.

"So *that's* why!" she said in a rushing whisper. "Five days, and he hasn't touched or looked at me. You'd have thought I had plague. Ever since it—And I thought he'd just been having fun with me! What does he think I *am*?"

"He wouldn't let you be dragged into this. And you said he was spoiled and in bad need of a fall, anyhow."

"Dragged in? Let him try and keep me out! The big, brilliant, incapable *idiot, how* did he get himself into this mess?"

"It's nothing to you, anyhow," pointed out Dominic, tasting a kind of slightly bitter but still unmistakable joy. "You wouldn't have him. You don't even like him."

"I know I don't. I could wring his neck! And anyhow, what do you know about it, Dominic Felse? The last time he asked me I didn't tell him yes or no, I just walked away." She had been all this time ricocheting about the room like an uncoiled spring, slamming the cover on her type-writer, grabbing her coat from a closet, sweeping the papers from the table into a drawer anyhow, just as they fell. "And now I'm walking back," she said, turning the blue blaze of her indignation on Dominic, as if he had dared to challenge her. "Whether he likes it or not. I bet he hasn't even got a lawyer. Can you get bail in a case like this?"

"I don't know, I'm just the errand boy." She had caught him by the hand and was towing him with her through the doorway; and there, caught close together, they turned to spare one hurried glance for each other, and she stretched across the remaining few inches, and kissed him on the mouth.

"With me, you're royalty plus! But right now, if you can drive, you're the chauffeur. I've just started lessons. Can you?"

"Yes, I've got a licence. But we can't possibly take——"

"We can, we're going to. We've got to get down there quickly. She's out with Benson in the Morris right this minutes, but the Rolls is in the garage."

"*Rolls*? Not likely!" gasped Dominic, appalled. "I'd be terrified to *touch* it. Suppose I went and scraped the paintwork?"

"You won't!" she said, commanding, not reassuring.

And he didn't. And perhaps that was all that was needed to crown this mad holiday with the right extravagant finale, the impossible fantasy of himself driving that glossy, purring, imperial monster doggedly and gloriously out of its garage and down through the steep, narrow streets of Maymouth to the square, with Tamsin bright and fierce as a fighting Amazon beside him, and parking it with the superb accuracy of sheer lunatic chance in a painted oblong only just big enough to contain it.

Tamsin patted his shoulder, and said something wild and fervent and complimentary, that he never even heard in his daze of retrospective terror, and was gone like an arrow across the square.

Dominic sat quivering with reaction, still clutching the wheel. He wasn't even sure he could stand up now, he thought his knees would give under him if he climbed out and attempted to walk away. They didn't; he got out, closed the door with reverent gentleness, tried a few steps, and had hard work not to take to his heels. One thing was certain, as soon as he turned to look again at the majesty on which he had just laid impious apprentice hands : the chauffeur would have to fetch it back. Nothing in the world would have induced Dominic to tempt providence a second time.

: :   : :

George, humanely withdrawn to the window of Hewitt's office, and thus having half the square in his sight, saw the resplendent car insert itself with the delicacy of desperation into the tight parking space, saw the brave red head sail flaming out of the opened door like a torch, and blaze across towards the doorway below him. And in a minute more he saw the driver's door open, and his son emerge. George's brows rose; he permitted himself a small, appreciative smile. Taking away cars without the owner's permission, now. No need to ask if Miss Rachel had been consulted. Dominic's charge-sheet was becoming interesting. But George was not an exclaiming man. The speaker and the listeners behind his back knew nothing of the storm-wind that was blowing rapidly their way.

Simon, having reached simultaneously the end of his cigarettes and the end of his story, felt lighter, but with the lightness of emptiness. If you can see your whole life clearly as you drown, so you can when events go over you like a tidal wave, and effectively drown the person you have been up to now. Simon saw his life as a dust-sheeted room, the occupant of which had gone gallivanting so often and so far that he had never actually had time to live in it at all. Such a lot of time wasted, looking elsewhere for the impermanent. He'd left it too late to realise the potentialities of a son, and far too late to fall in love with a girl twelve years his junior.

I'm a thirty-seven-year-old widower, he thought, looking into the last coils of cigarette smoke as into a mirror, and a pretty harsh mirror, too. I'm going to be doused head-first in the kind of publicity I'd rather do without, and I shall learn to live with it. I'm going to be hurt, and survive it. I'm going to be stripped of my privileges, and fight my way back into a competitive world as best I can. But at any rate, the distress to other people is only going to be marginal.

He offered himself this, despondently, as a worthy and comforting thought, but instead it made him feel even more depressed. It's too late for me to change, he thought, I've revolved round myself too long. Much the best thing I can do is keep my own company. No wonder I could never find the right note with Tamsin, no wonder I always managed to sound as though I was insulting her. I suppose in a way I was trying to protect her, wanting and not wanting, begging for her and warning her off. And Paddy —what was he to be? A consolation prize? Thank God they both have sound instincts. They know a heel when they see one.

The quietness of the room was suddenly shaken by raised voices below, one of them, and the one that seemed to be laying the law down most emphatically, unmistakably a woman's. They all pricked up their ears, Simon most sharply of all. But it couldn't be! She couldn't even know anything about it yet, and even when she knew, why should she interfere?

George crossed from the window; Hewitt rose from his desk in mingled irritation and curiosity, and stalked across to open the door and call down the stairs: "Who is that? What's going on down there?"

The tones which had disrupted the desk-sergeant's calm echoed imperiously up the well like a trumpet-call: "Oh, Mr. Hewitt! Good! I'm coming up." High heels pattered rapidly up the uncarpeted stairs like a scud of hail. "Is Simon here with you?"

Simon was on his feet, shaky and disrupted with hope and dismay, and an absurd, shamed apprehension; half hoping against his own heart that Hewitt would manage to send her away, half smiling in spite of his own conscience, because he knew that that was more than the entire Maymouth constabulary and the county regiment could have managed between them.

"You can't come up now, Miss Holt, I'm occupied," Hewitt blocked the doorway with a broad body and an extended arm.

"I *am* up. He is there, isn't he? What's he told you? What have you charged him with?"

"He hasn't been charged with anything yet," said Hewitt dryly. "He's made a statement, which is now being typed. And you've got no business here, my girl, let me tell you that." He had known her since she was a pig-tailed imp doing acrobatics on the swings in the

park; if he couldn't control her, he could still make satisfactorily stern noises.

"Oh, yes, I have. I bet he hasn't even done anything
about a lawyer yet. I want to talk to him. Let me in!"
Not a request, a command.

She appeared beyond Hewitt's solid shoulder, pale and
bright and formidably angry, her red-gold hair in ruffled
feathers on cheek and temple, her forehead smudged with
carbon. Her eyes, levelled lances, flashed across the room
and pierced Simon to the heart. Faint flags of colour
had come to life in his tanned cheeks, warming the grey
of sleeplessness out of them. An incorrigible spark of mischief reappeared in his eyes, a shadow of itself and veiled
in desperation, but alive. The two roused faces locked
glances like the beginning of a battle or an embrace.
Difficult to be sure which, thought George, edging un-
noticed towards the door. Maybe both.

The first words of love sounded like the clash of arms,
if that meant anything.

"You're a fine one!" said Tamsin hotly. "What the
devil have you been up to, to get yourself in this mess?"

"If it's a mess, at least it's my mess," said Simon, all
the more loudly and angrily because of the longing he had,
and knew he must suppress, to welcome her in and grasp at
this unbelievable happiness while it offered. "What do
you think you're doing here? For God's sake, girl, go
home and behave yourself."

"'Go home and behave yourself,' he says," Tamsin rolled
bitter blue eyes to heaven in mute appeal. "Listen who's
talking! And he isn't fit to be let out alone!"

"I doubt if he's going to be let out at all for the
next year or two," snapped Simon, man-alive again, and
surrounded by a live, thorny and rewarding world. "So
you can make your mind easy, *you* won't be needed for
a keeper. Now get out and leave me alone!"

Maybe it was the note of entreaty he hadn't been able
to suppress, or maybe she possessed an intuition that didn't
even need such aids. However it was, Tamsin knew her

moment. The blue of her eyes softened to its calmest gentian darkness.

"It's the forty years or so afterwards I'm worrying about," she said sternly. She looked at Hewitt, looked him levelly in the eyes, and smiled.

"You'd better let me in. Give me ten minutes with him. I have got a certain right here, you know. That's my fiancé you've got in there."

She had unfurled her colours, and nobody would ever be able to trick, bully or persuade her into striking them again. Seemingly they all knew it. She breasted Hewitt's large arm, and it gave before her and let her in. She looked as if she could have marched through walls just as irresistibly. She marched straight at Simon, all pennants flying.

"Ten minutes!" said Hewitt, and shoved George before him out of the office, and closed the door upon them.

THE END